THE MIDAS CAT 2

THE MIDAS CAT 2

ROLPH'S REVENGE PART 1

Tommy Ellis

Published by 3 Spot Press

Copyright © 2020 Tommy Ellis.

The right of Tommy Ellis to be identified as the Author of the Work has been asserted by him in accordance to the Copyright, Designs and Patents Act 1988.

All rights reserved. No part of this publication may be reproduced, stored in a retrieval system, or transmitted in any form or by any means without the prior written permission of the publisher, nor be otherwise circulated in any form of binding or cover other than that in which it is published and without a similar condition being imposed upon the subsequent purchase. All characters in this publication are fictitious and any resemblance to real persons living or dead is purely coincidental.

About The Author.

Tommy has been a full-time musician and entertainer since 1988 and writes in clubland and holiday park dressing rooms whilst waiting for the bingo to finish. He has two other Midas Cat books availalable from Amazon - The Midas Cat: The Devil Wears Tabby and The Midas Cat: The Harrington Collection, both of which have met with critical acclaim.

Praise for The Midas Cat series.

"Cleverly funny" - Louise cannon, arts critic for Bookmarks and Stages. Five stars

"An absolute gem. Five stars" - Amazon review

"Intelligent, zany, laugh-out-loud funny" - Amazon review

"This is excellent" - Kaylee Gryba, Canadian comedian and author of Single and Catless

"Rip-roaringly entertaining" - Amazon review

For Carwyn

TOMMY ELLIS

"In ancient times cats where worshipped as gods;
they have never forgotten this - Terry Pratchett.

PART 1:ROLPH'S REVENGE

CHAPTER 1

Ralph

Ralph ran a hand over his freshly shaved scalp as he stared at the monitor. He'd had to lose the custom made hairpiece due to infestation, but he didn't mind too much. It gave him one less thing to worry about.

He'd been released from Falcon Hall Secure Psychiatric Unit the previous week due to a computer error, having spent just over a month as a resident. His exclusive Caribbean holiday island had been cut off for days after a hurricane tore through the region, and when they'd found him he was screaming deliriously about a talking cat, and a voodoo death spirit.

They'd told him it was all in his head, but what did they know? They'd never met the midas cat!

Now he was free, he had things to do, though. There was a talking cat to capture and an ex-wife to win back.

Lauren's marriage to film director, Troy Halliday, had imploded after she'd caught him in bed with a downtown hooker who was dressed in a cat onesie. The divorce had been big news about a fortnight back. She was now rich: Tatler rich. Her lawyer had screwed Halliday for a fifty percent share of his production company. He'd also squeezed him for a twenty five percent cut of royalties from his blockbuster franchise, *Donkeyman*. What she didn't have, though, was a midas cat, and that was something she'd always wanted.

His inbox pinged. It was his online contact, Midascatman1. He had a midas cat for sale. OK, it wasn't the mega-rare wild breed worth in excess of one hundred million, but the domesticated version would have to do. So long as it could talk, what did he care? Three million quid was a bargain if it bought a way back into Lauren's life.

His plan was straight forward. He'd buy the cat, fly with it to LA where he'd contact Lauren. She'd be so overjoyed at receiving a midas cat, she'd remarry him on the spot.

He read and re-read the email. Then he read it again. Another buyer had promised to get the cash to Midascatman1 within the next forty minutes.

That gave him just over half an hour to get the cash and leave it by the litter bin next to the clock tower in Falconbourne town centre. Midascatman1 would then contact him with further instructions.

The problem, however, was getting hold of cash.

He'd accidentally inherited three million due to a typo in his uncle's will. His cousin Rolph was beyond livid, but so what! It had turned a fat profit but was tied up in stocks, bonds, and the insider-trading track. So, if he wanted actual money, he'd have to take out a short-term loan. There was only one place he could get his hands on that amount, however, and the thought terrified him.

He'd advised local *Cash-Flow-King,* Yanko Biddle, on tax avoidance schemes and saved him millions. He'd also got him laid. Even though Biddle owed him, he hated dealing with the odious little psychopath. Still, it would only be a short term loan. Once he'd liquidated his investments, he'd be able to pay the money back within a few days and, in theory, never have to see him again.

CHAPTER 2

The Cat

Cat loved carnival week. What with the dressing up and the food fayre in the High Street, it was one of her favourite times of the year. This year's celebration had already got off to a great start. She'd gate-crashed a posh fancy dress party the previous evening and had given an interview for a national TV channel. When the reporter had enquired about her realistic cat costume, she had wondered what the idiot was going on about. Costume? Makeup? It was her own fur and nobody *else's* face!

He must have been a bit thick because when she downed a pint of champagne and proceeded to give her undercarriage a good groom, he'd nearly fainted. Fuck knows why. She was a cat. That's what cats do.

The party had gone downhill after that with a whole lot of shouting and complaining, so she'd cleared the canapes table, washed it down with a couple of bottles of Dom Perignon and left. At least she thought she'd left. She may have hung around for a bit first, but she couldn't be entirely sure.

The morning paper had an amusing story, though. British actress Lisa Lovelock, who played the half-human, half-cat character Tabby McGill in the Donkeyman movies, had been sectioned under the mental health act for claiming to be a real cat on national TV. That was just stupid! She didn't look anything like a real cat. Apparently, numerous witnesses had seen her licking her backside and quaffing champagne straight from the bottle before jumping up onto the top of a bookcase and singing Adam Ant songs whilst waving a pair of realistic-looking flintlock pistols around. Some people could be so immature!

Cat stared at the pap-snap of the actress. The make-up and tabby body suit were obviously fake, but the height was about right. For a human, she was tiny. Four feet tall at the very most. With another fun-packed day ahead of her, though, Cat had other things to think about.

She pulled on her coat, holstered her flintlocks, and adjusted her tricorne hat in the mirror. Dressing up as a highwayman in tribute to her favourite pop star was genius. She was bound to be the only one. Long live Adam Ant!

She picked up her duffel bag and pulled out the pewter hip flask. Nineteenth century single malt from her sister's collection, lovely! She took a long pull and smiled as the complex mix of peat smoke and heather slipped over her gums and ignited a warm glow deep inside her. That would set her up for the carnival, pubbing, clubbing and a trip to Cambridge to meet up with her brother, Jimmy and her sister, Professor Yolanda Barnes. A midnight feast around the open fire in the prof's private university study was a tradition she didn't want to miss out on. She hadn't figured out how she was going to get there yet, but she wasn't worried as an opportunity for free transport was bound to present itself. It usually did.

She slung the duffel bag over her shoulder, checked her reflection for a final time and stepped into the September sunshine.

CHAPTER 3

Jeffrey

'Jeffrey!'

He hated being called Jeffrey. Jeff was better as it didn't sound quite as gommy. JD was cool, but Doctor Downey was by far the best. It *was* his proper title, after all. Doctor Jeff Downey, psychiatrist, and professor of experimental pharmacology. Working at the prestigious Falcon Hall Secure Psychiatric Unit should have afforded him at least a modicum of respect.

'Jeffrey!'

'Yes, Mother. What is it?' He tried to keep the irritation out of his voice which was becoming increasingly difficult. She always wanted him to do stuff when he was in the middle of something important, like mixing pharmaceuticals or conducting ground-breaking research.

'I can smell the cat's litter tray. You haven't

cleaned it out, have you?'

The pigging grit tray again? He'd only done it an hour ago. It couldn't be full up again, could it? 'It wouldn't be so bad if we actually had a cat, for fuck's sakes!' He knew he shouldn't have been so snippy, but how was he supposed to get the dosage right with his home-made drug-pistol darts if she kept interrupting him?

He Pushed his seat back from the kitchen worktop and sniffed the air. The usual background odour of mildewed damp no longer registered, but as he walked around the permanently twilit basement flat, he could definitely smell something. It was too sickly sweet to be drains and had the wrong tang to be rotting vegetables. Although, having thought about it, it could be the cabbage he'd misplaced last month.

'Sort it out, Jeffrey!' If you don't, you know what will happen!'

Jeffrey grimaced. What was likely to happen was a barrage of unending verbal abuse from the bedroom next to his. Even though Mother was now bed-ridden, her tongue hadn't diminished in either edge or power, and why she didn't allow him to block up the cat flap was a mystery.

He raked at the wood pellets revealing nothing. If the local tomcat hadn't popped in for a shit, then what the hell *was* that smell? He shook his head. Whatever it was, it wasn't something he could do anything about.

'Have you done it, Jeffrey?' Mother's schoolteacher voice drilled into his long term memory and struck oil. Going to the same school your mum taught at wasn't conducive to a happy childhood. Especially when she insisted on asking him if he'd remembered to put on clean undies in the middle of the school assembly. She'd actually called them *undies,* as well, and that was the end of life as he knew it. His nickname from then on had been *Skidmark.* Not good when you're sixteen years old.

'Yes, Mother, I've done it.' If she'd just shut the fuck up and let him get back to work, he'd have enough ammo to shoot the midas cat and the bloke who was selling it and have a few darts left over just in case. Then he'd have his very own talking cat. He'd be on TV doing talk-shows and interviews. Hell, with a midas cat he could have his own programme, or maybe a movie franchise like Donkeyman.

He had it all planned. After discovering what Ralph Williams was up to in Falcon Hall's computer room, he'd become hooked. Knowyourmidascat.com had given him exactly what he needed. A shortcut to serious money. Midascatman1 wanted three million quid in cash dropped by the litter bin next to the clocktower in Falconbourne. Not a problem. He'd skimmed Falcon Hall's petty cash for enough notes to make it look as though there was a bagful of twenties and he'd packed out the rest with cut up pieces of thin plastic.

'I'm going out for a bit.' He knew Mother wouldn't approve, especially with it being carnival week as well, but he had to assert his independence. Hell, he was a bloody doctor. If that didn't give him the right to go out on his own every once in a while, what did?

'Not during carnival week, you're not!'
He'd heard that particular sermon countless times over the years. Anything that resembled fun was strictly forbidden because it could lead to debauchery and a weakened mind.

Before Mother could wind up the lecture machine to its full devastating potential, he slipped out the door, closing it quietly behind him.

As he walked up the steps to street level, he went over the plan one last time. Drop the bag of fake money, hide down the nearby side street, follow Midascatman1 when he shows up, shoot him and the domesticated midas cat with the drug gun, and then steal one of the world's only talking cats. Yep, that was a plan.

CHAPTER 4

Eric, The Conman Previously Known As Rolph

Another buyer? He already had his thieving scum-bucket cousin on the hook and now some other gullible loser was willing to donate to his retirement fund. He never realised being Midascatman1 could be so profitable.

Things had been looking up ever since he'd changed his name. Rolph. Who the hell was named Rolph? It had hardly brought him fame and bloody fortune, had it? If he'd been named Eric in the first place, the typo in his father's will wouldn't have made any damned difference and he would have already been three million up. Six million quid in one day was more than he deserved, though. Actually, when he thought about it properly, it was the least he deserved for having his inheritance stolen from him by his shit-eating relative. If he conned

Ralph out of three mil, he'd be a happy man. If he conned another moron who'd come along for the ride too, well, whose fault would that be? His for the con, or the moron's for falling for it? Three million was good, but six million was better. If it worked, he might be able to pull it off again.

His plan was simple. Put the Donkeyman carnival costume on over his normal clothes, break into the clocktower in Falconbourne using the key he stole from the council offices and watch the litter bin from the window beneath the clock. He'd figured it out a few years ago. People rarely looked up. They spent their lives looking straight ahead or down at the ground. Although, it had to be said, there was something to looking down with the amount of dogshit in the town.

Phone zombies were another thing altogether, though. Mindless mobile addicts strolling through fast moving traffic and knocking window cleaners off ladders. But still, it wasn't phone zombies he was on the look-out for, was it?

Once the bag, or possibly bags, of cash were dropped off, he'd wait for the mark, or marks, to leave as instructed, slip out the door at the clocktower's base and walk away into the crowds of carnival revellers at least three million richer.

Part two was the clever bit, though. He'd drift with the crowd until some of them visited the pub opposite the clocktower and follow them in. Then he'd nip to the loo, lose the costume, and emerge in jeans and an oversized sweatshirt with poachers pockets sewn into the double lining which would, of course, be stuffed with cash. He'd get himself a pint at the bar so as not to look suspicious before walking away into a long and happy retirement.

His inbox pinged. It was Doctor D, and he'd promised to deliver the cash in forty minutes. Eric's excitement levels spiked, making him want to piss, but he had to get into position, so he busied himself with the outfit before heading out into the warm afternoon.

CHAPTER 5

Ralph

Time squeezed him hard.

'Yanko. Hi, it's Ralph.' His grip on the mobile was so tight, it made his hand hurt. Forcing himself to relax, he glanced at the clock on the car's dashboard. There was no time for *how're the kids, nice day* pleasantries, so he got straight to it. 'Listen, I need a favour. I need a short term loan. Three million in cash.'

He was asking a psychotic loan shark to lend him three million quid. He knew it wasn't particularly wise, but he was on a tight schedule, and the clock told him he only had forty minutes before somebody else got his midas cat. 'Yeah, that's right. Three million. Cash. I'm good for it, and I'll really make it worth the investment.'

He put the phone on speaker and reversed out of his driveway. The silence coming from the other end of the line, however, made him wish he'd never asked for the damned loan in the first place, and he seriously considered hanging up. The old bastard always took so long to decide on anything, Ralph wondered how he'd become so successful. Then he remembered his penchant for breaking people's legs. Violence was a great way to make a person rich.

Another minute clicked by. If the scabby lice breeder took any longer, he'd be out of time and end up losing the cat *and* Lauren. 'Yanko, listen. I'm in a serious hurry here, and I need your help. Do you remember that Norwegian girl I set you up with a few years back?' He hoped he wouldn't have to make this play, but Yanko had left him with no choice.

'Yeah, that's the one. The one that washed out of the sewer overflow pipe a few days later. I've got footage of you in bed with her with a silk scarf tied around her neck.' There was no way back from that one, and if it went the wrong way, he may just as well go straight to the Co-op and start picking out coffins. 'Like I said, I'll really make it worth your while.' He hadn't checked his investments for weeks and hoped to hell he had enough to cover the promise.

'No, Yanko. Nobody will ever find out, and when I pay you back, I'll bring the flash drive...The *only* flash drive.'

He ended the call and accelerated hard. Yanko was camped out by the marshes on the far side of the industrial estate north of Falconbourne. If he put his mind to it, he could be there in five. That would give him just thirty four minutes to conclude his business and get to the clock tower. It was tighter than an undersized g-string but not impossible.

Carnival week was getting bigger every year, and fancy-dressers were everywhere. He glanced at a group of vampires and goblins crowding the pavement to his left. There was over a month until Halloween. Didn't any of the idiots own a calendar? He shot down Waterworks Road, loose chippings pinging off the car's underside.

Up ahead to the right was Quock's licenced restaurant and takeaway. He used to like Quock's special chow mein until The Department of Health closed the place down. Now it stood empty with corrugated iron hanging listlessly from the window. He backed off the accelerator just as a kid in a highwayman's outfit shot out in front of him. Was there some sort of stupidity virus going around? Halloween outfits in September and now this! Didn't its parents ever teach it road safety?

He slammed the brake pedal, and the wheels locked up, sliding on the newly laid surface. The car's back end swung out as the tyres lost their traction.

Always turn into a skid. That was the rule. He spun the wheel hard to the right, and the car jounced sideways up the kerb.

By the time he saw the lamp post, it was too

late. The phone shot across the dashboard, deconstructing itself on impact, and the airbag exploded as the side window shattered, showering him with a machine gun hail of flying glass.

A buggered car, a destroyed phone, and it was all that damned kid's fault! He scrambled across the centre console and kicked open the passenger door.

The kid stared at him. He was sure it had fur on its face. It was probably just his mind playing tricks on him due to concussion, or something. And why was the idiot clapping? He'd just had a near-fatal crash and the evil child was applauding him. Whatever the reason, he didn't have time to hang around and find out as the distant wail of sirens meant time here was at an end. Besides, the accident had burned through precious minutes that he could ill afford.

If he went through Waterworks Park, though, he could cut across country, make up for lost time, and, hopefully, be out of sight before the police arrived.

CHAPTER 6

The Cat

The pint in The Swan in Falconbourne town square had been the perfect pick-me-up. With the taste of hops still lingering on her tongue, Cat made her way up Waterworks Road towards the group of children. The sign in the town square had said something about street theatre, fancy dress competitions, a food fayre, and a grand parade. She'd already seen the grand parade and filled up her duffel bag with lobster, sweets and cake from the food fayre but wondered when and where the street theatre would be. She'd been to Florida and seen the Halloween Horror Nights in the theme parks. If it was anything like that, she'd be well happy. OK, it wasn't October, but pop-up theatre appearing in random places around the town was a fantastic idea.

'Hey, check it out!' The goblin with the spikey green hair was pointing at Cat. 'It's Tabby McGill from Donkeyman!'

Where had Cat heard that name before? She couldn't quite pin it down, so she just smiled and nodded.

'And the teeth!' Goblin-boy grabbed the half-sized Dracula. 'Here, Baz. Do them cat teeth look real, or what?'

Baz stared into Cat's mouth before pulling out his own set of plastic glow-in-the-dark fangs. 'I'll swap ya.'

What was the small primate jabbering on about? She could no more take out her teeth than she could take off her own head. What on earth were they teaching the monkey descendants nowadays? She shook her head and pondered her next move. She couldn't see any sign of the street theatre, and it was too early to head for Cambridge. She supposed she could always go back to the pub. As she weighed up her options, she spotted it. On the far side of the road was a place she'd been meaning to check out for a while. Quock's licenced restaurant and takeaway. Licenced meant booze and restaurant meant the possibility of grilled lobster. Lobster washed down with red wine. Why not? Cat nodded to herself as she skipped through the crowd of children.

'Oi, Tabby McGill!' It was the spikey haired goblin-kid. 'Where you off to? I thought we'd play a bit of knock down ginger.'

She wasn't going to get herself tangled up with anything dodgy like that. She shook her head and pointed at Quock's.

'Whoa,' said goblin-boy. 'Quock's? They'll never let you in there. It's for grown-ups only.'

Cat shrugged. She was a cat. She could get in anywhere. Before the kids managed to rope her into anything unsavoury, she darted across the road towards the eatery.

The sound of tyres losing their grip on loose chippings made Cat look up. A bald lunatic was struggling to regain control of his car and wasn't doing a particularly good job of it. The idiot had obviously been sampling the range of real ales in The Swan and was sampled off his head, as the vehicle had now mounted the kerb sideways.

Cat stepped neatly out of the path of the moron-mobile and watched as it slammed sideways into a lamp post. The accident was far better than any Hollywood CGI special effects. Cool! Exploding airbags, shattering glass, what's not to like?

Bald-lunatic-man crashed out through the passenger door and stared at her. Was he expecting a round of applause? Of course! What she'd witnessed wasn't an accident, it was the start of the street theatre. To be fair, she'd been expecting jugglers, buskers, and a bit of Shakespeare, but this was far better. It was like watching an action movie played out in the streets around her. Fantastic! She clapped and wondered why the kids hadn't joined in. Perhaps they didn't get it. Peasants!

Now that scene one was over, it was time for her

to move on. She reached Quock's and turned the handle. Nothing. She tried again before noticing the sign. *Closed due to food poisoning.* Oh well, she'd just have to go to the Falconbourne burger van. It served something called a kitchen sink, the biggest burger Cat had ever seen, and it contained everything except its namesake.

Before then, however, she had a promise to fulfil. The professor had asked if she could pop down to the marshes on the other side of the railway near the industrial estate. It was, apparently, a site of special scientific interest, but Yolanda didn't know if she'd be able to get her mobile laboratory over the railway crossing due to its size. She also needed to know if the ground was firm enough over there as she didn't want to lose another mobile lab.

CHAPTER 7

Ralph

The industrial estate was supposed to have been extended beyond the railway line into the marshes once they'd been drained. The council had even started building the flyover that was meant to link the Waterworks side of the tracks with what was going to be called The New Water Road Estate.

Ralph stood by the railway crossing, knuckles whitening as he gripped the edge of the closed gate. Truck after truck of an endless goods train had been rumbling past for about two minutes, but it felt longer. He hadn't seen a train on this section of track for ages, but that was just bloody typical, wasn't it!

He stared up at the remains of the flyover. He remembered when it had collapsed. The council had farmed the work out to an outfit that should have come with custom made Stetsons, and they'd neglected to drain the water off properly. That caused one of the concrete pilings to sink into the mud, which in turn pulled the central section of roadway with it, blocking the railway for over a year. The project was abandoned, costing the local government millions and the following year's election. The only way anyone was crossing that bridge now was on a rocket powered stunt bike.

The gates finally opened. No traffic ever came this far down because it was, technically, a dead-end. That meant he could walk in the middle of the road without fear of being run over. Except, of course, by old man Yanko and his sterile psycho-sons.

Yanko was dangerous, but Harley and Lemmy should have been given free room and board in Falcon Hall's D-wing. He'd always wondered how closely related Yanko was to his wife.

Up ahead, a group of three caravans, a flat-bed lorry, an ancient pick-up, and a brand-new Range Rover Sports encircled a blazing fire pit. Ralph stepped between the Range Rover and lorry and moved into the gear oil and smoke scented ring.

In the fading September light, the flicker of the campfire danced across the underside of the fly-over, and Harley stared unblinkingly through the flames.

'Where's Yanko and Lemmy?' Ralph glanced about. Harley was the only one there and that made him nervous. If either of the other two were out there in the shadows, that meant... Ralph buried the thought. He was here to borrow a shit-load of money and that was bad enough.

'The. Old. Man's. Busy.' The words were slow as if Harley had to formulate each one before opening his mouth. 'Sit.' He patted an upturned plastic bucket and grinned, gold teeth glinting in the dancing firelight.

'Where's Lemmy?'

'Hunting.' Harley grinned again before handing Ralph an open jam jar filled with a muddy brown liquid. 'Drink.'

Ralph knew the rules. If you're offered a drink, you drink it. Even if it was a pint of donkey piss. He lifted the jar but couldn't help sniffing it. Expecting a rancid stink, he was pleasantly surprised. The scent of warm cinnamon cut through the wood-smoked air. He nodded. This wasn't going to be so bad, after all. He took a deep swig. No warm cinnamon caressed his taste buds, just a sensation that burned one second and froze the next. A tasteless liquid that was pure torture ignited inside his mouth. If he spat it out, it would be considered an insult, so he swallowed hard, eyes streaming and insides convulsing. He gagged, a thin string of drool stretching from his bottom lip.

'Shit's got some kick, ain't it?' Harley slapped him on the back hard enough to hurt.

'You wait until the trip kicks in.'

Trip? Ralph's memory skipped to the kidnap attempt on the midas cat's sister and the effect the painkillers he'd taken at the time had had on him. 'What? This stuff's hallucinogenic?'

'Only kidding.' Harley back-slapped him again. 'The old man'll be out soon. This stuff gives him a liquid arse.' At that, he got up slowly and entered a caravan that was at least fifty years old and looked as though you could catch something nasty just by touching it. Loud music that could only be described as extreme death metal shook the mobile home so violently, small pieces of discoloured trim pinged off into the fire.

A car door slammed from behind him. He spun to face the sound just as a powerful engine rumbled to life. The Range Rover backed hard into a double-axle caravan and connected with a solid *ker-lick* before spraying dirt from all four wheels. What the hell?

'Harley, what the feck's going on?' It was Yanko. He was in the moving caravan and he didn't sound happy.

Ralph did a quick calculation that didn't make any sense. If Harley was in his own caravan and Lemmy was out hunting, who was towing Yanko away and why?

The car turned in a wide arc and headed straight towards the old viaduct. Whoever the hell it was behind the wheel was messing with some dangerous people and must have had a death wish.

As the Range Rover passed the fire, the driver's profile silhouetted briefly through the limo tinted window. The tricorne hat was unmistakable. It was the kid in the bloody highwayman's outfit! Not content with trying to kill him, the stupid bastard was trying to... He wasn't exactly sure what the kid was trying to do, but whatever it was, it wasn't sane.

The over-sized caravan bounced over the rough ground, the screaming inside becoming increasingly urgent. 'Harley! What the...' The screaming cut short as the car hit the decaying on-ramp with a thump, bottoming out the caravan. The car swung wildly to the left and the caravan pendulumed out behind it, catching on the central reservation. It tilted and held its position as the Range Rover straightened up and with a roar, lurched forwards. The van gave in to gravity and hit the road sideways with a sickening crunch.

Old man Biddle was in there, and there was a high probability the three million was in there with him. His three million, and it was heading off the edge of the flyover in thirty seconds unless he did something about it. If he didn't do anything, Harley sure as hell wouldn't.

The car had slowed to a crawl by the time Ralph had reached the caravan.

'Yanko, you all right in there, mate?' Ralph peered into the hole where the skylight had been. The old man was on his back, trousers around his ankles, portaloo liquid sloshing about the cubicle and he was blue from head to foot.

'Get me the feck out of here!'

Ralph reached for Yanko's hand and paused.

'What the feck are you waiting for? Where's Harley?'

Ralph glanced up. The kid had jumped. Not only out of the car but off the bridge. It had to be a twenty foot drop, at least. There was no way anyone could survive that. The kid's death was unimportant, though, because heading inexorably towards the ragged edge was the Range Rover pulling Chez Biddle. The kid must have set the cruise control because it wasn't stopping.

The car was way too close to the edge, and if he jumped into the driver's seat, he'd never stop in time before plunging to his death, so he had a choice. He could either save Yanko or the duffel bag with the wad of fifties poking out of the top that he'd just spotted nestling next to the skylight. Thoughts of presenting Lauren with a talking cat made his mind up. He snatched the bag just as the car's front wheels met empty air. The big V8 kept up its relentless grinding, the car vanished, and with a screech of metal on concrete, the old man's home followed.

The inevitable steel-tearing crunch made Ralph flinch, and he peered over the edge, afraid of what he might see.

The car was upside down on the railway tracks but was in showroom condition compared to the twisted pile of aluminium lying next to it. Yanko couldn't have survived the fall, and Ralph was about to turn around when a blue hand poked out of the wreckage.

Oh, Jesus. The tough old bastard was alive! He had to call the police, the ambulance, the fire brigade. He needed everything!

He plunged a hand into his pocket to pull out a mobile phone that, of course, wasn't there. It had been destroyed in the car accident caused by the fucking highwayman! Maybe Harley had a phone. He broke into a run just as a familiar two-tone sound cut through the evening air. The Euston express. He stopped sprinting as the reality of the situation ran him down. Harley was head-banging in his caravan, and Lemmy was out in the marshes somewhere. Ralph was the only outsider anybody had seen in the camp, so logically he was the one who must have killed Yanko. When Harley and Lemmy caught up with him, they wouldn't be taking him out to dinner.

The clocktower in the town centre told him he had a single minute left to make the drop. No doubt Midascatman1 was watching from somewhere nearby, otherwise how would he know who had made the drop?

He jogged to the bin and glanced about. Early evening drinkers, carnival revellers and fancy dressers were bunched in groups around the town square. Luckily, they seemed to be paying more attention to the food fayre stalls and burger van than to him. He dropped the duffel bag by the bin after looking inside it for a possible previous drop. There was nothing. He'd got there first. His instructions were to leave the cash, leave the area and await further instructions. Midascatman1 would know how to contact him.

He dropped the bag, but was he going to leave? Was he bog roll! He didn't trust Midascatman1 not to screw him, but he had to make it look as though he'd left. If it hadn't been pulled down, he knew the perfect hiding place. At the bottom of Woodgrange Road opposite the clocktower, was the old Headbat's brewery. Empty for decades and marked for re-development, it afforded the perfect view of the clocktower.

CHAPTER 8

The Cat

The industrial estate ended at the railway crossing. It was as if the council had run out of money because there was a bridge, a *coming soon* sign, and very little else.

Cat skipped across the line just before a goods train rumbled past. Then she followed the rutted track to a fork in the road. Now, what was it Yolanda had said? Was it left, or right? She looked both ways and, seeing nothing that freed up her seized memory, took the left hand path towards the flyover and the flickering glow of a campfire that bronzed the encroaching dusk.

Two men sat around a fire encircled by a mismatched selection of vehicles and caravans. The older of the two sounded as if he had some serious gut troubles. He tilted his moth eaten trilby back on his head before letting a long rumbling fart escape.

'Oh feck!' The trouser eruption sounded a bit too squishy to Cat. 'When will I ever learn?' The old man put the jam jar of brown liquid he was holding down on an upturned plastic bucket. Then he picked up a duffel bag that looked exactly like Cat's and, gripping his backside with one hand and the holdall in the other, shuffled towards the biggest and cleanest caravan. He opened the door and paused. 'Harley.'

Cat assumed it was the younger chimp's name.

'When the fecker gets here, tell him I won't be long.'

Harley nodded before taking a swig of the muddy brown liquid, squeezing his eyes shut and slapping his knee. 'That. Shit's. Got. Some. Kick.'

Cat frowned. What was wrong with the ape descendent? It sounded as though he'd missed out on some of the evolutionary upgrades. She'd learnt an awful lot from her sister, the most important thing being that you don't mess with anyone that hasn't downloaded the full complement of mental software. The professor never mentioned un-evolved monkey people living in the marshes. Surely, she wasn't studying them? She'd mentioned flora and fauna, but this lot were neither. She thought for a second. It was back at the fork in the road. She must have taken a wrong turn. It was time she left.

She was about to slip away into the shadowed evening when a familiar figure stepped into the ring of firelight. It was the stunt driver from earlier. What was *he* doing here?

'Where's Yanko and Lemmy?' For a stuntman who'd just trashed a car, he sure looked nervous. He glanced about the campsite, and his eyes shone with something more than trepidation. If someone popped a crisp packet behind him, he'd load his pants.

'The. Old. Man's. Busy,' said Harley in his slow, measured monotone. 'Sit.' He patted the upturned plastic bucket, and when he grinned, the smile didn't quite reach his eyes. He reminded Cat of a gold toothed shark.

'Where's Lemmy?' said the bald actor as he squatted down on the bucket.

'Hunting,' said Harley. Hunting? Cat glanced behind her, just in case Lemmy was in the bushes somewhere.

Harley gave the actor another of his shark grins before handing him the jam jar. 'Drink.'

The bald man sniffed the diarrhoea-coloured liquid, nodded, and took a deep gulp. His eyes bugged out as if he'd swallowed acid, and he gagged, a line of spit dribbling from his bottom lip. Was he going to puke all over Harley? Cat craned forwards. This was getting interesting. There could be a fight. If there was, her money was on Harley. He looked about as stable as antique dynamite and would destroy the bald actor in seconds.

'Shit's got some kick, ain't it?' Harley slammed an open palm down in the centre of the actor's back. 'You wait until the trip kicks in.'

Trip? Cat didn't get it. Neither of the men were actually going *anywhere.*

'What?' said the actor. 'This stuff's hallucinogenic?'

Cat nodded to herself. *That* kind of trip.

'Only kidding.' Harley smacked the actor's back once again. 'The old man'll be out soon. This stuff gives him a liquid arse.'

No kidding. The old boy shat himself just by letting a fart squeeze by.

Harley rose from the log he was seated on and ambled over to a leprous caravan that hadn't seen a sponge this side of the millennium and disappeared inside. Brain rattling music erupted that was so loud, it shook bits of trim loose. The death metal music gave Cat an idea, though. She needed to get back to town, and with the light draining from the day, she could make her escape without being seen or heard. The thing was, though, she didn't fancy walking. The brand new Range Rover Sports, however, would be the perfect vehicle to borrow.

She slid around to the car and checked the door. It wasn't locked. What were the chances?

Cat loved new-car smell. She breathed deeply as she reached for the ignition. Smooth V8 power burbled from under the bonnet. Nice.

She scanned the interior. Automatic gearbox, air con, cruise control, sat nav, an onboard computer more powerful than NASA and parking cameras.

Parking cameras? She wouldn't need those. She was a great driver!

Stuffing in her earbuds, she cranked Adam Ant's Greatest Hits, selected R for reverse and floored the throttle.

She howled along as the big 4x4 dug in. A solid *ker-lick* underscored the music. That wasn't on the track. At least it wasn't earlier. Still, with computer downloads and all that, anything was possible.

Shifting the lever to D, she pushed her paw all the way to the floor and the wheels slipped, sending up a spray of dirt and debris before gaining traction. Circling the fire, she decided the quickest way out was over the top. She was going to take the flyover.

Mirror, signal, manoeuvre. That was the rule. What was the point, though? It wasn't as if she was on the main road, or anything.

The actor stared at her with an unhinged mouth. God Knows why? Hadn't he seen quality driving before?

Accelerating towards the on-ramp, the Range Rover bounced and crunched over the rough ground. For such a powerful car, it wasn't pulling very well. Perhaps it needed a service.

She dropped the shift down to three and, with a thump that bounced her very nearly to the headlining, hit the slope. There was definitely something wrong because as soon as she turned the wheel to straighten up, she lurched to the left.

It might have been a nearly new car, but the damned thing had been abused something awful to behave in such a way. The rear end swung sickeningly. Cat tutted. The bloody suspension was shot as well as the engine. She floored the peddle in an attempt to gain a bit of speed up the incline and the car leapt forwards. The extra momentum was short lived, however, when a loud crunch came from the car's tail. That must have been the rear springs giving out. Maybe she should have borrowed the lorry instead?

Cat thought for a moment. Revving the piece of crap didn't seem to have much of an effect apart from making bits fall off, but if she switched on the cruise control, the horrendous beast would do its own thing.

The engine growled as the car crawled steadily upwards. Good. It seemed to be behaving itself. Cat looked back to the road ahead. Where had it gone? The bridge ended abruptly. It was as if it had snapped off, leaving a jagged edge. Well, that just wasn't on, was it? She'd have something to say to the council on Monday. Useless tossers!

The car was obviously in poor shape, so trusting the brakes wasn't a good idea. She opened the door and looked down. The road was going by at a relaxed enough pace for her to skip out. The only problem was the edge. It was getting nearer every second. The drop must have been about twenty feet. She'd launched herself off various tall buildings over the years and always landed on her feet, though. She was a cat. She was born to this! If her aim was as good as she thought it was, she'd land on the far side of the tracks beyond the bushes.

She glanced back at the bridge and pulled up short. Where the bloody hell did that caravan come from, and why was it lying on its side with the actor looking in through the skylight?

She shrugged. Not her problem. Then she jumped.

CHAPTER 9

Jeffrey

He checked his watch against the clocktower. He only had a single minute with which to deposit the carrier bag full of fake twenties, but it was enough.

He strolled through the town square, watching the early evening carnival goers and fancy dressed children. Why were a group of them dressed in Halloween outfits, though? It was still only September. Idiot kids!

He looked back at the litter bin by the clocktower's base. The drop point. Leave the bag and nip down Woodgrange Road. The old Headbat's brewery was still there and undeveloped. Hide, follow, shoot, steal. Simple.

'Oi, watch where you're going!' He'd been so focussed on the bin; he hadn't seen the group of adult fancy dressers. He'd shoulder barged a 1920s gangster who hadn't registered in his peripheral vision. He fought the urge to reach under his sweatshirt where the drug-dart gun he'd borrowed from work was wedged into his belt. One shot would do it, though. Especially with his customised mix of opioids, hallucinogens and… other stuff.

'Oh, sorry.' He had to remain calm and not draw attention to himself. If he got into an altercation, he'd run out of time and lose his chance at worldwide fame. Not that he wasn't already famous in the field of psychiatry and pharmacology, but he craved the acceptance of the wider world.

When he looked up again, he saw him. Ralph Williams had appeared from the far side of the clocktower. The duffel bag must have contained the three million quid and Midascatman1 would have seen him make the drop. Bugger! What was he going to do now? His hand went automatically to the pistol. He could shoot him. If he shot him twice he'd overdose and die. Midascatman1 couldn't sell the cat to a dead man, could he? No. He mustn't think like that. He was a doctor, not a murderer.

As the indecision locked his thought machine, he spotted something. He squinted to make sure he was seeing what he thought he was seeing. Coming around the opposite side of the clocktower was a child dressed as a highwayman. It wasn't a child, though, was it? He was sure he could see a pair of glassy green eyes shining out of a tabby and white face. If Ralph left the way he came, he might not see the midas cat. The pictures on the internet didn't do it justice. It was more magnificent than he could ever have imagined. In his mind's eye he could see the book cover, talk shows and enormous bank balance. He hoped he was right, though. If it was just a kid in a Tabby McGill mask... He pushed the thought to one side and the pistol back into his waistband. He didn't need to drop off the fake cash. He could get the cat for free if he played it right.

The carnival crowds had grown as the people from the parade floats joined the throng. He could use them as cover. Mingle, and when they drifted towards the clocktower, he could grab the animal. Shove the pistol into its back and it'd do exactly as he told it, just like the movies.

If he struck up a conversation with one of the carnival people, he could circulate more freely. Be part of the crowd instead of some hanger on. The woman standing by the market stalls gave him pause, though. She had her back to him, but he'd recognize that angular frame anywhere. Mother's near fleshless fingers gripped a Tupperware box which made him feel sick. His entire childhood had been dominated by clear plastic boxes filled with cold roast dinner sandwiches, and a large bottle of junior stomach pills. As if eating week-old leftovers wasn't bad enough, he'd had to suffer the indignity of carrying around a bottle that may just as well have said *I've got the shits* on it in bright pink letters. He wouldn't have needed the damned pills if he didn't have to eat rancid food in the first place, though, would he? It couldn't be her, though, could it? She'd been bedbound for the past year.

He had to get his head back in the game, so he closed his eyes, counted silently to five and opened them again. She'd gone. Maybe she'd never been there in the first place. He didn't have time to mess around with ifs and maybes, though. He had work to do.

'Nice outfit, especially the hat. You look just like a smurf.' He thought the young lady looked stupid, but he had to start somewhere.

'Ooh, ta. Do you like my smurf shoes as well?' She stumbled on a pair of overstuffed cartoon feet that probably started the day off as white but were now a dirty grey. Jeffrey's reflex action kicked in just in time, preventing her from face-planting the pavement.

'Thanks,' she said.

Things were going well. He'd saved a girl from an embarrassing fall whilst copping a feel. Although touching up a smurf was an offense that hadn't quite made the statute books, he mustn't allow it to distract him from the mission. He re-focussed on the bin. Ralph was walking towards Woodgrange Road without a backward glance, whilst the midas cat rounded the clocktower from the opposite direction. It was standing by the bin. It was standing next to the duffel bag full of money. Two for one! A midas cat *and* three million in cash!

'Oi, mister!' What did Smurfgirl want now?

'This is my fiancé, Duncan.' Duncan was the scariest smurf he'd ever seen. He must have topped out at six feet six. If they ever did a monster smurf, this guy was it. He just hoped he hadn't come to batter him.

'You saved Chanel from trippin' up.' Duncan grinned, cracking the blue face paint, making him look even scarier. 'Nice one, geezer.'

'No worries.' The phrase hid his true feelings. He had a list of worries. Being found out feeling up Monster Smurf's girlfriend was quite high on that list. 'You do what you can, eh?' He had to get back to business. 'Gotta go.' He stepped out from the milling crowd and froze. Where was the cat? The bloody thing had vanished!

He stared about, hoping for a glimpse of frock coat or leather boots. Nothing. The duffel bag was still there, though. At least he was three million quid to the good. He didn't have a talking cat, but at least he was now rich.

He scooped up the holdall and frowned. It didn't feel right. Something about its heft was off. He dropped the carrier bag of fake twenties, uncinched the duffel's opening and peered inside. His head spun, but he didn't blink. If he blinked, he might faint. Food? He reached in a hand and pulled out a gift-wrapped lobster. Something glinted from amongst the fairy cakes, though. Maybe the three million wasn't in cash. Maybe it was some sort of valuable antique. Made sense. Easier to carry. He plunged back into the food fayre haul once again, fingers searching out the artefact. He touched something cold and hard. And familiar. He hoped he was wrong. He hoped and prayed to all that was holy that he was wrong. He wasn't.

The pewter hip flask shone orange in the sodium streetlight. He turned it over and felt the liquid slosh about inside. He dropped the bag. What the hell just happened? Where was the money? And where was the midas cat? The hip flask slipped from his fingers. His plans had been torpedoed by the creature he was making plans for!

CHAPTER 10

Eric, The Conman Previously Known As Rolph

He was right about the phone zombies. If he'd have shot one of them, not a single virtual person would have lifted their head from their mobile virtual world. The first thing they would have known about it would have been through social media, even if they were the ones who'd been shot. That meant breaking into the clocktower whilst dressed as that stupid superhero, Donkeyman, couldn't have been easier.

There were no stairs up to the clock, only a manky wooden ladder that creaked with every step. Maybe he should have chosen a different lookout? The platform at the top was made from warped planks and several of them were missing, giving him a dim view of the pile of broken market stall frames he'd land on if he put a foot wrong.

The old Victorian mechanism stood silently on its cast iron framework, superseded by a near-silent electric model. When he got his cash, he'd buy the old clock workings. They'd make a great centrepiece for his penthouse apartment.

The leaded window just under the clock afforded him a perfect view of the bin. It was the *only* window, though. If Ralph came from the opposite direction, he wouldn't see him until he was standing right next to it.

He pulled the costume's head off to get a better view. Kids and adults in fancy dress mingled in the town square, but there was no sign of his thieving cousin anywhere.

He looked up. According to the clock, Ralph only had a minute left before the other mark, Doctor D, arrived. Ralph did want a midas cat, didn't he? Lauren had better not have been winding him up about the arse-wipe's obsession. If she had, though, there wasn't a lot he could do about it.

He looked down. Ralph had arrived and after rifling through the bin for a few seconds, he dropped his duffel bag, as instructed. Great! All he had to do now was leave and await *further instructions.* The only instructions he was going to receive would be the ones telling him what he could do to himself and exactly how hard.

Ralph was doing what he was told. He really was leaving. Eric shook his head in disbelief. Something in his life was actually going to plan. He'd be rich in about two minutes.

He watched his cousin disappear from sight. He'd gone towards Woodgrange Road, although God knows why as it was a dead end with nothing but a rehearsal studio and a derelict brewery.

He was about to pick up the donkey head when a kid dressed in a highwayman's outfit stepped into view from the other side of the clocktower. The kid was wearing a tricorne hat, had an identical bag to Ralph's and placed it on the floor next to the three million.

Oh, Jesus, the bastard kid was going to switch the bags and walk off with the cash. What the hell was going on? He had to get down there before the kid nicked his money.

He stepped towards the ladder, foot plunging through a gap in the planking. Falling forwards, he grabbed the window-sill just before his head hit the glass. His foot had jammed solid and it was all because of the stupid hooves on the ridiculous Donkeyman outfit. Why didn't he go as Prince Charming? At least he could have worn normal shoes! He stared down at the kid as it pulled something from the bag. It looked like a hip flask. What was the kid, seven, eight, maybe nine at the outside? Nine-year-olds don't own hip flasks. This was getting a bit weird. He pulled on his jammed hoof, whilst not taking his eyes from the kid.

The kid took a long glug, but try as he might, Eric couldn't see the face under the hat. Not to worry, though. Dressed as a highwayman, the kid wasn't hard to miss.

He tugged on his hoof again, sending debris clattering and pinging off the broken market stall detritus below. Sodding Donkeyman!

He hadn't been watching the window. Instead he'd been pre-occupied with freeing himself. He looked down. The kid had vanished, and there was only one duffel bag.

'Please, God, let it be the right one,' he whispered to himself as he braced for another tug. The stupid costume could have cost him his inheritance, and he wished, once again, that he'd worn something more sensible.

He heaved, his ankle digging into the warped plank. If it gave suddenly, he could end up flying over the edge of the platform and impaling himself on the rusty ironwork below. There was three million quid down there, though. What was he going to do, leave it for someone else to find?

The sharp crack echoed off the cobwebbed brickwork as he flew backwards. His hands scrabbled uselessly at the empty air as he hit the planking and slid towards the edge. 'Oh shit, oh shit, oh shit!'

Fingernails screeching, they blackboarded across the wood. Another gap in the planking. Fingers snatching at the splintery edge. Whiplash braking. He'd stopped.

His head hung over the musty emptiness, but he was alive. His heart hammered at borderline coronary level, but he didn't have time to waste. He pulled himself upright and carefully stepped over the gaps towards the window.

The kid had gone, replaced by a middle-aged bloke in a baseball cap who was carrying a supermarket *bag for life.* He'd always wondered about that phrase. Bag for life? Whose life, the bag, or the person? He shook his head to free the irrelevant thought. The man had dropped the bag, spilling what looked like twenty pound notes onto the flagstones. That's when it registered. Doctor D. He didn't look much like a doctor, but he'd brought the money. That meant that he, Eric, the conman previously known as Rolph *such a disappointment* Williams was now, if not filthy but relatively uncleanly, rich.

Once Doctor D left as instructed, he'd nip down, swipe both bags of cash and initiate part two of the plan. Six million meant proper comfort. No more faking it with rented Ferraris. He'd buy one.

Doctor D had picked up the duffel bag. That wasn't right. He'd given him strict instructions. Leave the money and bugger off immediately. Why was he rummaging around in the holdall?

Doctor D then pulled out a gift-wrapped lobster. Lobster? He felt like crying. It was the kid's food fayre haul. He was three million down, but at least he still had Doctor D's cash. Well, he would have if the sodding doctor did as he was told. His frustration built as the doctor dug a hand into the bag once again. There was no cash, that was obvious. So what was he up to now?

'Why don't you just fuck off, so I can get rich?'

Eric muttered to himself whilst willing the doctor, if indeed he was a doctor, to leave. When he pulled a hip flask from the duffel bag, Eric knew for certain he'd been stitched up. The only problem was how? His cousin had appeared, dropped the cash and left. He really wanted a midas cat. He wanted one so badly, he was willing to trust somebody he'd never met to deliver the goods after leaving a bagful of readies by a litter bin, just like a kidnap plot in a second-rate cop show. So who was the kid with the identical duffel bag?

The bag of food hit the flagstones, followed shortly after by a clank as the hip flask came down after it.

The doctor wore an expression a bit like Gollum when he discovered his invisibility ring had gone. His head darted about as if scanning the crowd for something.

Eric squinted through the dirt-caked window. The doctor had sprinted across the square. Mad as fuck! At least he'd gone, though. Eric put the Donkeyman head back on and carefully descended the ladder.

There were still plenty of people on the street, but not as many as earlier, and luckily none of them were anywhere near the clocktower. There was Doctor D's bag of cash, and as he stepped towards it, he knew instantly that he'd been conned. There were wads of twenties, but only the notes on the outside edges were real. The rest were cut up pieces of thin plastic. There was maybe a hundred quid in the bag, and that was being optimistic. Lying next to Doctor D's bag was the kid's hold-all, on its side, spilling cakes and seafood onto the pavement. There was no three million. Just a bundle of fake notes and a hip flask.

He picked up the flask, popped the lid and sniffed. He knew quality malt when he smelled it. Rare highland scotch, and as he tasted it, he realised how rare. If he had the bottle, he'd be holding at least a grand, but a dribble in a flask? He tilted his head back and drained the contents before scooping up the genuine twenties. Barely enough for a decent piss-up! What else was he going to do, though? He pocketed the cash and headed for the pub on the far side of the square.

CHAPTER 11

Ralph

The old Headbat's brewery was still there and derelict, but it now stood behind an eight-foot-high wooden hoarding topped with razor wire. There was no way he was getting in any time soon. He had to find a different place to hide, so he ducked in behind a rust-pocked Transit van. Luckily for him, the streetlights didn't work this far down Woodgrange Road and afforded him the cover of darkness. He could wait and watch. See what Midascatman1 was going to do next and follow him. Well, he had to make sure he was getting what he'd paid for.

The thing was, though, he hadn't paid for anything, had he? He may not have actually killed Yanko, but he'd taken his three million quid before leaving him to play chicken with the Euston Express. The thought churned his insides every time it surfaced. He tried to suppress it and concentrate on the clocktower, but it was no use. For what it was worth, he might just as well have shot the old bugger.

Biddle's kids would be out looking for him. That wasn't good. The sooner he concluded his business here, the better.

He looked up the road and focussed on the duffel bag. That's when he saw the kid. The damned highwayman that had caused so much shit tonight stood next to the bag of cash. Fucking kid! If he ever got his hands on him, he'd give him a thrashing he'd never forget.

He stared hard at the kid and felt his entire body lock up. It had a tabby and white face. He hadn't been seeing things earlier. The kid did have fur on its face because it wasn't a kid. It wasn't even human. It was a midas cat. A midas cat! A genuine, honest to dogshit midas cat! That meant he hadn't been stitched up. Midascatman1 was showing him proof of his sincerity.

The sounds of the evening faded as Ralph zoned in on the domesticated talking feline. It was going to happen. He could see it all. He'd get a message from Midascatman1 to meet him in a lock-up garage where he'd be presented with Tiddles. Then the rest of his life would just fall into place. LA, Lauren, and Lauren's billions.

His eyes watered. He hadn't blinked in nearly a minute. The cat had put its duffel bag down and had pulled out a hip flask before taking a long swig. He couldn't believe it. He was getting his old life back!

The cat put its hip flask back in its bag. It wasn't just *the* cat anymore, though. It was *his* cat.

A scuffle broke out amongst the fancy dressed carnival goers giving the cat pause. It glanced up and Ralph followed its gaze. A man in a baseball cap had saved a female smurf from taking a dive. He was sure the bloke grabbed her arse as he helped her up, the cheeky sod! He looked harder at the man. There was something that jangled a bell somewhere at the back of Ralph's mind, but it just wasn't jangling loud enough. He'd seen him somewhere before but where? It didn't matter, though. What did matter was covered in fur and dressed as a highwayman.

Ralph's heart was disco dancing with excitement. The domesticated midas cat stood not more than a hundred metres away and would soon be his. All he had to do was be patient. Eyes on the prize as his father used to tell him whilst administering a dose of the behavioural adjustment slipper.

It wasn't a con, so all he had to do was await further instructions. He could do that. He watched his very own talking cat pick up its duffel bag. Christmas was never as exciting as this, even when he was a child. Considering the presents he got, though, it was hardly surprising. The Bumper Book of Algebra, Corporate Law for Dummies and hand knitted mittens on string. Not the kind of things a six-year-old wants to find in his stocking.

As the cat sauntered away, Ralph's reverie was shattered by a familiar voice.

'Hello, Ralph.' The fake poshness that overlaid the broad, heavily nicotined estuary was unmistakable. Doreen had been the only carer at Falcon Hall who hadn't tasered him, but that didn't mean she wouldn't.

'Turn h'around slowly and put your hands where I can see them.'

He'd been given access to the patient computer, a heavily monitored system for the more *with it* inmates. Being an ex-banker, though, meant he knew his way around software, so arranging his own release hadn't been a problem...Until now. He raised his hands and turned around.

'Stay calm, Ralph. Stay h'exactly where you are.' He could see Doreen's bloated cheeks dimple as the sparking taser lit up her grin. She must have weighed in at a solid twenty five stone, but she had a stun gun in one hand and a drug-dart pistol in the other. Rumour had it she was an ex-special forces sniper. Ralph didn't know if that was true, but he didn't want to find out.

'You'll only make it worse for yourself if you h'run.'

Run? What other choice did he have? She may have been a crack shot, but she smoked like an unlicensed minicab. All he had to do was make it to the end of the road, and he could hide amongst the crowds.

He turned to face the clocktower and launched

himself forwards.

'Fuckin' stand still, ya shit!' All poshness had vanished as the first of the drug darts whirred past his head. If she got him, he was finished.

CHAPTER 12

The Cat

The town was buzzing, and Cat was ravenous. The walk from the marshes wasn't too bad but even so, it would have been better if she could have driven. Still, the Range Rover was a piece of junk. It was obviously mistreated and would have been an embarrassment, so letting it drop over the edge of the knackered flyover was a kindness. She'd put the poor thing out of its misery.

Before grabbing a burger, though, she fancied a quick nip of scotch, so she headed for the clocktower. She could sit on one of the benches and quaff whilst people-watching.

No benches. The council were hopeless. First of all they build a rubbish bridge, then they take the benches away. She'd definitely be on the phone first thing Monday morning.

She slipped her duffel bag from her shoulder and

placed it next to the litter bin. That's when she spotted it. It was a holdall identical to hers. She frowned as her memory did its thing. She'd seen that bag somewhere before but where? Unable to access the requisite mental software, she stopped trying and pulled her hip flask from her own pack, popped the lid and took a hearty glug. Her sister's collection of rare single malts was amazing, and this one she'd borrowed was particularly fine. 19th century highland whiskey salvaged from the wreck of The Titanic. Gorgeous!

She slipped the flask back into her bag and glanced up. A scuffle had broken out amongst the crowd of fancy dressed adults. Scuffles were good, as they usually ended up as a proper fight. Proper fights were a great spectator sport. None of your pushing, shoving and name calling, but a full-on knock-down, hair pulling, blood spattered punch up.

A bloke in a baseball cap had grabbed a lady smurf's backside. That was bound to lead to violence. It usually did. Cat waited for the first blow, but it never arrived.

He wasn't groping her; he was saving her. She'd stumbled, and he'd prevented her from headbutting the pavement.

Disappointment flowed to the ends of her whiskers when she realised there was to be no smurf fighting. Bloody shame!

She scooped up her bag and set a course for the burger van. She'd only taken three paces when her ears pricked up. A posh woman was ordering someone to put their hands up. This sounded interesting. Maybe it was some more street theatre. She turned to face the voice and way down Woodgrange Road she could just make out a couple of figures. One looked a bit like that bald actor she'd seen earlier, but she couldn't be completely sure, and the other one was a huge woman armed with a sparking taser and a pistol. Cool!

The woman fired her pistol just as the actor made a break for it. Her first shot missed, and the actor sprinted as hard as he could towards the clocktower. This was fantastic! Cat didn't realise street theatre could be so exciting. That was it! She was going to buy tickets to see The Lion King or maybe Cats. The actor ran on but stumbled when his left foot twisted inwards, sending him sprawling onto the pavement. When Lard-Lady ambled up to the actor and zapped him with her fake stun gun, he even pretended to piss himself before Lard-Lady picked him up in a fireman's carry and shoved him into the back of an old Transit van. What a performance. Bravo!

Now that the show was over, she turned her attention back to the acquisition of food. She'd tried everything in the burger van. It was all good, but the *kitchen sink* was the daddy. Two quarter pounders, bacon, cheese, a foot long hot dog, mushrooms, two fried eggs and a deep fried Mars Bar all encased in a small cornbread loaf.

'Oi, Tabby McGill.'

Her thoughts of burgers were cut short. It was Baz and his mates.

'How's it going?' said the Dracula kid. 'We're all a bit bored now. The carnival's finished and none of us are old enough to get any booze.'

Bored? How could they possibly be bored with the fabulous show going on all around them. She'd seen a live version of *The Hills Have Eyes*, a stunt car smash-up and just a minute ago she'd witnessed a fantastic abduction. These kids weren't paying attention!

''Ere Tabby, have you seen our mate Liam?' said Baz, the green haired goblin. 'He's got the same outfit as you. He's got the highwayman's hat, boots and everything.'

'Although,' said Kid-Dracula, 'yours does look better, and I love the old pistols. They almost look real.'

Almost look real? They *were* real. Genuine 18th century flintlocks, owned by Dick Turpin and borrowed from the professor's private collection.

Cat had had enough of the mini-chimps. She'd gone to huge effort to wear an outfit that nobody else would have thought of, and a monkey-person goes and copies her. Typical!

Her stomach growled. It was time to eat, so without a word she stepped away from the kids. The burger van was calling, but just leaving the queue with a *kitchen sink* was the other highwayman. Kid-Dracula was right, though. His outfit was by far the more inferior one. Plastic pistols and a foam tricorne hat. He grinned at her as he headed towards Baz, Dracula and the others. Peasant!

CHAPTER 13

Jeffrey

The cash had vanished along with the midas cat. The thought did a full circuit of his mind before fact number one caught up with fact number two. The cat had gone. The money had gone, the three million having been swapped, somehow, for a bag of food and a hip flask. Did the cat have a duffel bag? He wasn't sure, but if it did, it could have switched out the cash for a pile of fairy cakes and a lobster.

The situation wasn't good. It was looking more like the plot of a bad spy movie every second; two identical bags; put down one; pick up the other. The cat must have known about the money, or why would it have been carrying an identical holdall? He'd lost the cat and the three million quid. He'd failed...again. Mother's voice screeched in his head. *You'll never amount to anything unless you apply yourself, Jeffrey!* He cringed at the imagined onslaught but braced for what was coming. *Oi, Skidmark! Show us your undies!* His classmates had latched on hard to that one phrase, and it was always followed by the new school song. Simple lyrics, and a simpler tune made it easy to remember, unfortunately. *Show us your undies, show us your undies.* Then he'd get wedgied.

That was the only reason he'd applied for the job at Falcon Hall in the first place. He had to show the world he was successful. Doctoring was the perfect career and psychiatry was the perfect fit. He knew more about the defective mind than most. Hell, he'd lived with Mother his entire life!

If he had a talking cat and three million quid, he'd be more than just successful, though. He'd be rich and famous. The problem, however, was not seeing the cat anywhere. The midas cat had the money. That meant if he could find the cat, he'd also find the money. Win, win.

He scanned the town square and zoned in on the burger van. It was Mother's doppelganger again. OK, it wasn't actually her, but in his heightened state of awareness, he was likely to see all sorts of things. Including talking cats? No, that bit was real. It was, wasn't it? He had to throttle back on the anxiety pills.

Redoubling his concentration, he forced himself to think logically. Where would the cat go? It was the size of a child and wouldn't really fit in with a group of adults. Therefore it was either in the pub, which was unlikely but possible, at the burger van with Mother, or hidden amongst the gaggle of children. Not wishing to find out if Mother was real or not, he'd start with the children.

'Hi, I'm looking for...' He never got the chance to finish the sentence because the spiky haired goblin kid cut him off.

'Fuck me, it's Skidmark. My dad told me all about you.'

A nerve in his face twitched uncontrollably. As much as he wanted to locate the midas cat, he wanted to kill the little goblin even more.

'My dad told me that your mum was head of the old Falconbourne Comprehensive. He said that you shat yourself during assembly, or something, and your mum told the whole school.'

The sniggers from the rest of the crowd erupted into full-blown laughter, and Jeffrey had to will his hand not to snake beneath his sweatshirt.

'Yeah,' said the child in the Dracula costume. 'I heard that you're an inmate of Falcon Hall. Locked up coz you killed your mum.' He turned to the rest of the mob. 'The loopy fucker never forgave her. Chopped her up with a bread knife and stuffed her down the drain.'

'No! It's not true!' She wasn't dead, just bedridden, and the smell was probably a dead mouse that bloody tomcat had brought in.

The laughing stopped instantly, and the kids backed away. 'Told you he was mad,' said Dracula.

'I'm a doctor. I work at Falcon Hall. I'm...I'm...'

The words jammed in his head as Goblin-boy spoke up.

'You ain't no doctor. You empty the bins and sweep up shit.' He pointed a finger at Jeffrey. 'My dad does deliveries to Falcon Hall, and he's seen you.'

He *was* a doctor. He saw patients in the refectory of Falcon Hall every day, *and* he had access to the dangerous drugs cabinet.

As he walked away, he could hear the old school song start up from behind him. *Show us your undies, show us your undies.* He had to get away from the children before his willpower collapsed, and he started shooting. Besides, he had a midas cat to catch, and it wasn't amongst the kids. That left the crowd by the burger van, the food fayre stalls, or the pub. The animal had obviously been to the food fayre already because of the haul of grub in its bag. Which to choose, then? The burger van, or the pub? The burger van was nearest, and besides, he'd have a clear view of the pub's front door.

The crowd was thick, and the food smelled delicious. If it wasn't such an important mission, he'd have definitely ordered something. How to spot a midas cat in a crowd, though? He couldn't just rifle about in the queue, could he? He'd most likely get thumped. Then he remembered what the stupid thing was wearing. Highwayman's hat, breeches and boots. The boots! All he had to do was look at people's feet.

He took a step back. Trainers, shoes, more

trainers, but no riding boots. The only thing left was to ask someone. 'Excuse me.' The 1920s gangster pointed the plastic tommy gun at Jeffrey and in an unconvincing Chicago accent said 'you lookin' at me?'

'Yeah, sorry. I'm, err, looking for a highwayman. It's my nephew and he's late home.' He thought the nephew bit was inspired and made him seem less dubious.

'A highwayman?' Al Capone reached for the biggest burger Jeffrey had ever seen. 'Yeah, mate,' he said in his normal voice. 'He just got a burger and went to join that group of kids in Halloween costumes.'

Sorted! The only problem was the kids. He didn't fancy going through the humiliation all over again, so what was he going to do? He could always use the drug-dart pistol. With a whole carnival floatful of gangsters carrying toy guns, one more weapon wouldn't stand out. Shoot the cat, grab the money and walk away whilst propping the damned thing up. He could always say his nephew had had too much to drink.

CHAPTER 14

Eric, The Conman Previously Known As Rolph

He'd lost everything to his thieving, undeserving, shit-smeared cousin. What he wouldn't do to him right now if he thought he wouldn't get caught trying to scam the bastard. Something slow and excruciating involving fire and a hammer drill, maybe. Still, the unhinged pervert would probably enjoy it.

Eric shuffled towards the pub on the far side of the town square, Donkeyman hooves scraping on the pavement. He stopped when a familiar name was called from behind him.

'Hello, Ralph.' It was a woman's voice. Estuary with an overlay of obviously put-on poshness.

He turned around. With the Donkeyman head on, he had to physically turn his whole body in order to see behind him. The damned head was virtually impossible to see out of. It had two mesh grilles where the nostrils were, for both seeing and breathing through, and every time he moved too fast, the head slipped either sideways or downwards. That made the negotiation of crowds, kerbs and street furniture more than slightly hazardous. He'd already tripped on a cracked paving slab, walked into a litter bin and pushed over Smurfette, the latter nearly earning him a pounding by the biggest and scariest smurf he'd ever seen.

He'd take the head off, but he knew if he did, Ralph would recognize him and suss out that the whole domesticated midas cat thing was a con.

Also, Doctor D was still around here somewhere and didn't know what he looked like, and he preferred to keep it that way.

He focussed on the woman's voice. It was coming from Woodgrange Road. He pulled the head up to give himself a clearer view. It wasn't perfect, but through the mesh he could see Ralph getting tasered by an enormous woman before pissing himself and getting slung into the back of an old Transit van. Had he been kidnapped, or something? If he had, Eric hoped she'd start removing digits before the day was out. 'Good,' he muttered to himself. 'I hope he suffers before dying in agonising pain.'

He turned away and was about to make for the pub when an idea landed. Ralph had dropped a duffel bag full of cash by the bin. Or at least he thought he had. When the kid arrived, he had an identical holdall. He then dropped it and walked away leaving a bag of food. Also, the kid was on foot, so unless he caught a bus, a cab, or got a lift, he couldn't have got far. If there really was three million in that bag, the kid now had it, and he was probably still in Falconbourne somewhere.

Sonofabitch! There's a bloody 8-year-old kid wandering around with the most expensive food fayre haul in history, and he probably doesn't even realise.

All he had to do was find the highwayman and take his duffel bag. If he offered Doctor D's cash for it, was the kid likely to say no? Not for a bag of cakes and a lobster he wouldn't, surely?

Right. Sod the pub, it was time to catch a highwayman.

CHAPTER 15

Ralph

Feeling had come back to Ralph's limbs, and he wasn't sure if that was a good thing or not. He was strapped to a gurney in the back of the Transit van he'd hidden behind earlier. A psychiatric ambulance disguised as an old beater was genius. It could be used to track down escapees without alerting them to its presence. Of course it was a good idea. It had worked on him, hadn't it?

'Oh dear, Ralph.' Doreen loomed over him with a too-big syringe in her hand. 'The IT department discovered your little plan. Faking your h'own release form h'isn't clever.'

Ralph had thought it was. He'd got out, hadn't he?

'Do you really think you'd be able to hack our system without h'us knowing h'about it?' She squirted a clear liquid from the end of the needle.

'Thirty CCs of quiet juice should sort you out.' She leaned in and rolled his left sleeve up to the elbow, the harsh fluorescent light glinting off the droplet clinging to the spike.

'Time for beddy-byes.' Doreen's face broke into what Ralph supposed she thought was a warm smile but was closer to a smug grin. 'Then you'll wake in the nice warm comfy room.'

The *comfy room* was code for the padded cell. He'd spent a day in there as a new arrival. Twenty four hours of continual light with nothing to do and nothing to read.

If he wanted his old life back, he had to act now. He bucked and thrashed in his constraints and felt his right-hand wrist shackle give. In her haste to strap him down, Doreen hadn't done up the buckle properly.

'Come-come,' said Doreen. 'There's no need for that.'

Yes there bloody was. He yanked hard at the loose strap and the buckle jangled as his hand shot out and gripped Doreen's arm. Ralph knew he had to use every second of his advantage before the big woman's realisation circuits kicked in. If he could inject her, maybe he could bring her down.

'Ya sneaky fucker!' Doreen pulled free with no more effort than it would have taken Ralph to pick his nose. 'Right!' She raised the syringe in a dagger-grip intent on stabbing him with it. 'All privileges are hereby revoked!'

It was over. He was finished. The fat lady hadn't

started singing yet, though, had she? Ralph bucked and his left leg lightened suddenly. A dull clonk registered at the edge of his hearing, and his footless ankle shot upwards. His prosthesis had come off, leaving nothing holding his leg in place.

Doreen groaned and doubled over as Ralph's stump drilled into her stomach. Advantage, Williams. The game wasn't over yet, though. He reached across and pulled at the restraints on his left wrist. He had to free himself fully and inject the old cow before she recovered.

Incoherent mumbling came from the van floor. He'd really done the business but mustn't dwell on it. If she got to her feet, it would all be over.

Only his right foot to free up and he was sorted. He reached down, and that's when he saw it. Still full and un-plunged, the syringe had landed next to his right foot. Gripping the vial between his teeth, he worked on the final restraint just as the permanently curlered head appeared over the gurney's edge.

'OK, ya little shit!' Doreen's face was a shade above burgundy with slightly darker spots high up on her slab-like cheeks, and she looked murderous. Unlike Ralph, though, she wasn't armed with a syringe full of *quiet juice.* He stabbed the needle into the soft folds of her neck and pushed the plunger home. Her face blanked, and she slumped to the floor. Game set and match to Williams.

He freed his right foot, replaced his false left foot and hopped off the gurney. He should really strap Doreen down, but there was no way he'd manage to lift that much dead-weight without rupturing something. Heaving her onto her back, Ralph rummaged through her pockets. Another hypo. Perfect. With the extra bulk she was carrying, she'd need a larger dose and a second shot should just about do it. Once she came around, though, she'd be out after him, and he'd need something to defend himself with.

If he took the drug pistol, it would look obvious tucked into his belt and he'd probably get arrested. The taser, however, was much smaller. It was pocket-sized and far easier to stash.

Snapping the key off in the ignition, he ripped a handful of wires from under the dash to disable the van and stepped out onto the Falconbourne streets. It was time to go midas cat hunting.

The town centre was still full of carnival goers, which meant the domesticated midas cat could be there somewhere. He'd paid for it. OK, not with his own money, but nonetheless it *was* paid for, and that meant he owned it. If he spotted it, he'd be within his rights to take it.

At least he knew exactly what he was looking for, though. The damned thing was dressed as a highwayman. Surely there wouldn't be anyone else looking like a cross between Dick Turpin and Adam Ant, and as he surveyed the square, he knew in an instant he was right. There it was, trying to mingle with a group of kids. Even with its back to him, he just knew it was the cat.

He had to be swift. Spin the creature to put it off balance before tasering it to subdue it. Then he'd have it *and* Lauren.

He gripped the cat's shoulder. It didn't feel right. His intuition screamed, but it was too late to take any notice of.

Taser in hand, he spun the highwayman to face him. Staring at him from over the top of the biggest burger he'd ever seen were a pair of eyes, but they weren't midas cat eyes.

'What the fuck?' The mega-burger spun from the boy's hands, splattering across the paving slabs. 'Get your paws off me, you creep!'

Why hadn't he paid attention to his intuition? If he had, he wouldn't be doubled over in testicular agony with a knee buried in his groin.

'You touch me again, you nonce, and I'll get my dad to sort you right out!'
The kid didn't need any help from his dad. For a nine-year-old he was doing a fine job of it all on his own.

'Go on, Liam, finish him off!' The juvenile Dracula almost bounced up and down in anticipation of bloodshed.

'Nah,' said Liam. 'I know what he looks like now. That means if I ever see him again...'
The kid wasn't going to kill him. He'd got away with it. Got away with it? The lad wasn't even into double figures and had successfully crippled him. He needed to shape up.

He stumbled away from the group of jeering children, and through his tear-blurred eye saw what could only have been a tricorne hat. He blinked to clear his vision. The boots, the hat, and the coat. It was a highwayman. There were two of them. If Liam was behind him, that meant this one had to be the bloody cat. He couldn't be absolutely sure, though, because the face was obscured by another of those blasted burgers. He dug his knuckles into his one good eye and tried to focus.

Peering over the top of the portable heart attack were a pair of glassy green eyes, and weren't those things whiskers sticking out either side of the burger? He'd found it, and all he had to do now, was go and get it.

He tried to straighten up, but the devastating pain deep in his guts hadn't quite let up. There it was, only a few feet away, and he was hobbling along like Quasi-fucking-modo. It was definitely the cat, though. Because now he'd had a chance to re-order his thoughts, he realised it had a duffel bag. The midas cat owned a duffel bag. He knew this because he'd seen it. The cat had pulled a hip flask out of it. He nodded to himself. He was back on track but wouldn't be if he didn't keep up with it.

It was sauntering away, but in his present state he could barely stumble after it, let alone saunter. He had to try, though, because if he didn't, he'd never get back to the life he deserved.

As he wrenched himself upright, he spotted the

man in the baseball cap. The shifty looking bugger had saved Smurfette from taking a dive and here he was again, but this time Ralph was sure he knew who he was.

It was during his stay at Falcon Hall. There had been a caretaker. Yes, that was it. He used to talk to the inmates as if he was some kind of psychiatrist. The real doctors hadn't paid him any attention. Not until he'd been caught with his hands in the restricted medication cabinet, at any rate. All they had to do was medicate the mad fucker and not let him out, but because he worked for less than minimum wage, they'd let it slide. Jesus! Still, he didn't have time to worry about that right now, did he? He had more important things to do.

His innards finally let go of the breath-stealing agony, and just as he straightened up fully and was within only half a dozen steps of grabbing the talking cat, a firework cracked, and he spun to face the sound. The bastard kids were letting bangers off in the street. He mustn't allow the irresponsible shits to distract him now he was so close.

He turned back to his prize when a second firework went off. Fucking kids! A ricochet zinged past him, and he ducked. Roman candles don't ricochet. Somebody was shooting at him, and he had more than a rough idea who.

'R-Ralph, y-ya f-f-fecker!'

He knew the voice, recognized the stutter, and if he hadn't already have pissed himself, he would have emptied his bladder on the spot. 'Lemmy?'

'Y-yeah, y-ya m-murdering sc-scum.'
Ralph zoned in on the voice. It was Yanko's *Wrong Turn* duo. Lemmy, dressed in his customary rancid 70s pinstripe over a torn Donkeyman tee-shirt, held a pistol. The black revolver gripped in his oil stained fingers couldn't have been any bigger than a 22, but bullets are bullets no matter what the calibre.

'Guys, listen to me.' He had to talk them down because he knew nobody was coming to help. If you hid in the shadows trying to mug people, you'd get arrested for looking shifty. Do it blatantly in the middle of a town centre during carnival week and nobody would give a shit. 'I didn't kill your dad. It was…' It was who? He'd seen the kid dressed as a highwayman in the car that pulled Yanko to his death but only in profile and only from behind limo tinted windows. Why would the kid risk his life nicking the Biddle-mobile?

That's when the truth opened its big glassy green eyes. 'It was the…' What was he going to tell the hair-triggered lunatic? A legendary talking cat killed his father? 'It was…' That's when he saw it. Strolling along behind the Biddles, face still obscured by the enormous burger, was the domesticated midas cat. It was right there, looking at him, and he was sure it was smiling behind that artery clogging sandwich of death.

'It. Was. Who?' Harley had finally caught up with the conversation. That would make talking the pair of them down just that bit harder. Harley always seemed to be half a step behind everyone else. That meant if Lemmy decided not to kill him, Harley would have still been digesting the order to shoot, and by the time his brain caught up it would be too late. How the hell was he going to get out of this one?

'It, it...' His thought engine misfired as he spotted the bonkers caretaker again. He was stalking the cat. *His* cat. The bastard was about to steal his domesticated midas cat, and there wasn't a thing he could do about it. 'You have to...' *Listen* was what his next word was going to be, but his sentence was guillotined as the cat darted across the road followed by the caretaker.

The screaming tyres and bang-crunch of a multiple pile-up caused Harley to turn and face the action. The caretaker lay sprawled across the bonnet of a car with a green light on the roof. A doctor had run him over, the cat had vanished, and Lemmy hadn't even blinked.

CHAPTER 16

The Cat

It was spectacular. The biggest burger Cat had ever seen and filled with an amazing assortment of meat. How do you eat a burger that was nearly as big as your head, though? She could barely see over the top, but what she *could* see was that bald actor. He was striding towards Baz, Liam, and the others. This was probably some sort of interactive scene.

When the actor grabbed Liam and spun him around, she was sure he'd jump. That would serve the peasant right for copying her outfit. The actor held the fake taser that Lard-Lady had used on him earlier. That was sure to scare the junior monkey.

Liam's burger spun from his hands, splattering across the pavement, but he wasn't scared of the actor in the slightest. Bloody shame! Instead, he swore at the poor bloke before kneeing him in the groin and stealing his taser. It was still a good show, though.

She took a bite of hotdog and watched as the bald actor staggered in her direction. Oh well, that part of the show was over and obviously hadn't gone according to the script. It was time she found somewhere peaceful to finish her supper, anyway. She hit the play button on her iPod. A bit of Adam Ant was just the thing to help her find a quiet nook.

She strolled across the square taking in the carnival atmosphere. There were some fantastic fancy dress outfits. There were 1920s gangsters with tommy guns, smurfs, clowns, Hawaiian hula dancers, but her favourites were the actors playing their roles as psychotic swamp dwellers, and there they were. The scene in the marshes was brilliant, especially when the older one pretended to shit himself. The old guy was nowhere to be seen, though, but the younger one was right there. She sifted through her memory and found what she was looking for. Harley. That made the other one Lemmy.

This was going to be a good scene because she had just spotted who the swamp dwellers were homing in on. It was the bald bloke. It was getting better, as well. Lemmy had drawn a gun and had fired off a couple of blank rounds. No doubt the police had been informed, otherwise this sort of thing would never be allowed.

The bald actor looked genuinely terrified. It was as if he thought he was really about to die. If there were awards for this art form, then he'd be in line for an Oscar. Once the show was over, they'd all be off down the pub together, no doubt. Thoughts of the pub reminded her. There was a quiet car park behind The Swan where she could finish her supper.

Adam Ant's *Puss in Boots* kicked in as she skipped across the main road. There was no point waiting because nobody ever stopped, anyway.

Just as she reached the far pavement, sound effects of a massive pile up blasted through her ear buds. Why there was a car crash sound effect on this particular track, she had no idea, but she nodded in appreciation. It was definitely something new. When she got home she'd google her hero to find out more.

She burped and wiped a paw across her mouth. *The kitchen sink* was amazing but had left her feeling thirsty. That meant there was only one thing for it. The rear entrance to The Swan was a mere dozen steps away. It was time for a pint.

CHAPTER 17

Jeffrey

So the highwayman had joined the group of kids, had it? That meant the midas cat was less than twenty feet away. If he got this right, he'd be three million richer and on the jetway to superstardom in less than five minutes.

He scanned the group. There was the vampire and the goblin and there, at the edge of the crowd, was the highwayman. He had a clear shot, and if one of those nasty children got caught by a stray dart, so what?

The cat had its back to him which meant it wouldn't see him coming. The thought of a bagful of cash and his own TV show was almost too much to comprehend. All he had to do was not miss.

He lifted the sweatshirt's hem and wrapped his fingers around the pistol's grip. After the first shot the cat would go down, and once the kids realised the reality of the situation, panic would sweep through them. They'd scatter, leaving him with enough time to collect his prizes and melt into the ensuing mayhem that would, no doubt, infect the entire town. Nobody would realise that he'd caused the mayhem, though, because the gun was silent. He'd just look like he was helping a drunken kid.

He had to be quick, though. He couldn't stand, arm outstretched, for too long, could he? Well, it would look a bit dubious.

Extracting the gun carefully from his waistband so as not to shoot himself in the leg, or worse, he drew a bead on the animal. Line up the sights, exhale gently and squeeze.

From this distance he couldn't miss. The pressure he exerted on the trigger was slight but firm. Count back from three and fire. Three, two… What the hell? Somebody had not only cut across his sightline, they'd grabbed the midas cat as well. He'd never get a clear shot now. If he got a bit nearer and changed trajectory, maybe. He took a step to the left and that's when Ralph Williams spun the cat. It had to be that fucker, didn't it! That was the shot, though. Right there! Shoot the cat, shoot Ralph. The enormous burger spun from the cat's hands, exploding in a shower of grease and meat as it hit the pavement.

Squeeze a bit more and… Hands? He'd seen the burger fly out of a pair of hands, not paws.

'What the fuck?' The voice wasn't feline, and as he zoned in on the face, the truth battered him.

The boy in the highwayman's outfit slammed a knee into Ralph's groin, doubling him over. Jesus, that was close. He'd nearly wasted a dart on the wrong target.

'Get your paws off me, you creep!' The lad was raging. 'You touch me again, you nonce, and I'll get my dad to sort you right out!'

If that wasn't the midas cat, then where the bloody hell had it gone? He stuffed the dart gun back into his waistband, slid into the doorway of a closed TV shop and watched Ralph stagger away from the children.

His competition was focussing on something, and when he followed his gaze, he realized exactly what. He'd grabbed the kid in the highwayman's outfit because they'd both made the same mistake, that's why. The hat, boots and frock coat were almost identical, as was the huge burger. The whiskers sticking out either side, however, weren't. No wonder they'd both got it so wrong. This time, though, the cat was his if he could get another clear shot.

He eased out of the doorway as the animal sauntered away. If he didn't keep up with it, it could slide out of his grip. Just because it could be seen, didn't mean it could be caught.

He took no notice of the firework that cracked off to his left. When the second one ricocheted, however, he paid attention. That was no firework. There were two lads in their twenties that didn't look normal. OK, with all the fancy dress costumes around today, normal was a moot point, but these guys were out of place even amongst the smurfs, donkeymen and gangsters. One wore a crusty suit that hadn't seen a drycleaners for a decade, whilst the other one should have been a permanent resident of Falcon Hall. The most worrying aspect, however, was Scabby-Suit-Boy's pistol. He was pointing it at Ralph, though, so on reflection, he had nothing to worry about. If Ralph got shot and killed, he, Doctor Jeff Downey, would get the midas cat. Whatever Ralph had got himself mixed up in wasn't his concern, so long as they finished him off.

Scabby-Suit-Boy had gone into one and was waving the gun around. That ought to keep Ralph occupied whilst he went after the midas cat.

The cat was ambling along behind the Crusty-Brothers as they homed in on Ralph. It was dawdling which was perfect. A nice slow-moving target. This was his chance to shine, and he reached, once again, for the dart pistol. He could almost taste the success the cat would bring him.

Without a glance left or right, the cat propelled itself out into the fast moving traffic. What the hell was it doing? It flowed, unharmed, between the cars and disappeared. If he didn't want to lose it, there was only one thing he could possibly do.

The screeching tyres and burning rubber meant he'd failed. He glanced to his left just in time to see the green light on the car's roof. How fucking ironic. A psychiatrist being run down by an on-call doctor.

CHAPTER 18

Eric, The Conman Previously Known As Rolph

The bloody Donkeyman outfit was a serious impediment. The oversized hooves had a habit of turning inwards making him trip over his own feet, and as for the damned head, not only was visibility virtually nil, it was hot, too. If he took the outfit off, though, Doctor D would know who he was, and so would Ralph. That would ruin part two of the plan. Although, it had to be said, his genius idea was starting to look a bit tatty around the edges. What use was the disguise if he couldn't find the bag of cash?

He'd been stumbling around Falconbourne for ages when a banger exploded off to his left. Kids were chucking fireworks about, and if one came his way, he'd never be able to dodge it before it went off. He doubted the costume was up to European fire safety standards, and that meant he'd be better lit than the bloody streetlights.

A second explosion was followed immediately by a zinging ricochet and a dull thunk just above his left ear.

A ricochet? Only gunshots do that, and as for the thunk, it was too soon after the shot not to be anything other than a bullet hitting its target. Hitting him!

His head flew around to where the shot came from, but the donkey head stayed stubbornly in place, giving him a perfect view of the neat hole in the costume's skull.

Oh shit! Some psycho was using him for target practice. Whoever it was had shot him once. He was still alive, but for how much longer?

He set off at a stuttering jog, each breath filling his lungs with the coppery tang of fresh blood. He'd been shot in the head! He'd been shot in the head, and he was still moving. Where the hell was the bullet, then? Was it lodged in his brain waiting for him to jostle it loose and kill him with a massive haemorrhage?

As he ran, the sound of a dried pea in a cardboard box rattled around inside the donkey head. It was worse than he thought. A bit of his skull had been blown off and was bouncing around his ears. He was lucky to still be alive, let alone upright. He had to do something now if he didn't want to bleed to death in the street.

Donkeyman's face grinned up at him as the outfit's head hit the paving slabs. He could clearly see where the bullet had gone in. A perfect circle had been punched just below the felt covered left ear. That meant the left side of his skull must have been missing. He reached a trembling hand expecting to find a devastating life-changing wound.

'Ow!' He flinched as his fingers explored his scalp. No exposed brain sponged under his touch, but his hand came away wet with sticky redness. Well, it would have been red in the daylight but was more a polished brown under the orange sodium glow. It was only a graze. If it *was* only a graze, what was rattling about inside the outfit?

He wiped a blood smear from his left eye and knelt beside Donkeyman's overly happy face. Sitting in a congealing blood-pool was a flattened lump of lead, confirming his fears. He really had been shot and had to get out of there.

When he looked up to figure out his escape route, though, the tricorne hat, boots and frock coat drove all thoughts of death-by-sniper out of his mind. He'd found the highwayman. He'd found his three million.

If he could get to the kid without falling flat on his face, it would be a bonus. What would he do then, though? He could hardly deck him and steal the cash. He'd have to play it differently. He could say the duffel bag was his, and he'd lost it. No. Kids are savvier than that. The bag had three million quid in it. He could offer him a reward of a grand. That was a lifetime's worth of money to a nine-year-old. Yes, that's what he'd do.

He must have looked a state with his face caked in blood. Luckily, it was carnival week. Everyone would just think it was makeup. Or at least he hoped they would.

He gripped the boy's shoulder. 'Here, kid. I need to...' His sentence was snipped off as his jaw slammed shut and his entire body spasmed.

'I told you to keep your fucking paws off me!' The voice and face were well known to him but as the thousand, or so, volts crackled from one end of his nervous system to the other, he barely had the capacity to remember his own name.

The deadbolts holding his legs up sheared off, and the kid zapped him again just before the pavement rushed up and kissed him roughly on the forehead.

'Liam, it weren't the bald bloke.' One of the kids was speaking and through the burned-out circuits of his mind, Eric picked out one word, and that one word struck more terror into him than some random maniac who was using him for target practice.

'Lum?' Getting tasered not only buggered up his thinking, it screwed with his speech centre as well.

'What did you fucking call me?' Liam's face lit up blue as he reached down with the spitting stun gun. 'Hold on.' Liam paused; the arcing electricity close enough for Eric to taste the bitter ozone raking at his throat.

'You're Rolph from next door.'

'Yeb. Me Wolph.' There was still some serious power outages going on in his brain, and Rolph couldn't remember his new name, let alone pronounce it. He knew he had one, but he just couldn't grasp it. Was it Eddy, Egbert, or maybe Englebert? At least his limbs were coming back online, though.

'Yeah, ya tosser. I can see that now.' Liam's monobrow creased in the middle. 'Why you dressed as a blood-soaked Donkeyman, and more importantly, why'd ya grab hold of me?'

Pins and needles lit up every nerve ending as Eric struggled to right himself.

'Oh no,' said Liam. 'You're staying down until you tell me what's going on.' He ignited the taser and held it close enough for Eric's hair to stand on end. 'You're the second nonce to grab hold of me tonight.'

'Where's da bag?' Eric's mouth was starting to feel as though the tongue that lived there actually belonged to him.

'What bag?' Liam shook his head. 'Nah, you ain't changing the subject. I don't know any bag. And besides, it's me what's asking the questions.'

'Duffel bag.'

'I ain't got no duffel bag. Besides, only a div uses a duffel bag.' Liam screwed his face up. He looked constipated, but Eric assumed he was concentrating. 'What's it to ya?'

'P-p-p...' The circuitry hadn't quite made contact, and the harder he tried to say *please*, the worse his speech became. He hoped it wasn't permanent.

'P-p-p?' Liam looked skyward for a second as if seeking divine help before locking onto Eric with a stare that could only be described as evil. 'P-p-p-porn.' The grin that erupted across Liam's face gave the unsettling stare the added dimension of gleeful menace. 'D, you hear that, lads? The pervy bastard's lost his bag of dirty mags. That's gonna cost him!'

The un-dead crowded in, the stun gun illuminating their made up faces an eerie blue-white.

'He ain't gonna want anyone to know about this, is he?' said Liam. Head shakes and muttered confirmations came from the mob.

'If my dad ever found out about this...' He let the sentence hang, but Eric didn't need it spelled out. Liam's father, DCI Frank Stone was head of the flying squad. He was an old-school hard bastard, and a throwback to the so called good old days of the 1970s. Whether Eric had done anything wrong, or not, it didn't matter because the pint-sized extortionist had learnt from the best.

''Ere lads. How much d' ya think it would be worth for me to keep me gob shut about all this?'

Dracula's fangs glinted in the sparking taser light. 'Gotta be a grand, innit?'

Oh, Jesus. He hadn't even located the bag of cash, and it had already cost him a thousand quid. If he didn't find the money, what then? 'I've only g-got a t-t-tenner on me.' His tongue was finally coming back under his own control, as was his memory, and the rest of his body. If he made any wrong moves or noises, though, the evil little shit wouldn't hesitate to light him up again.

'A tenner, eh?' Liam rubbed a hand over his chin as if in deep thought. It was so convincing; it was almost as if he could think beyond fags, booze, and blackmail.

'OK, call it a down payment. Trust me.' He straightened up and nodded. 'It'll be a sound investment.'

A sound investment? Had he been on a ride-along with Daddy?

'I want the first hundred by Monday or I'll send my dad round. Capiche?'

Did he really say *capiche*? The nasty bastard was a bent-cop-cliché-in-waiting, and Eric knew it was pointless trying to explain his way out of things. Still, at least he'd remembered his new name. Besides, what was worse, a bag of porn, or a bag of cash? It had cost him a grand, and Liam thought the duffel only contained rude pictures. If he found out the truth, he'd probably demand a fifty percent cut.

'Monday, all right?' Liam pointed the arcing taser at him as if it were a gun. 'Don't forget.'

Eric laid on the pavement and watched as the evil dead ambled away. So much for his new name being lucky. A kid dressed as a highwayman had nicked the money, he'd nearly fallen to his death in the clocktower, he'd been shot at, tasered and blackmailed. He needed a drink.

He yanked off the stupid Donkeyman hooves. He wasn't getting his deposit back, anyway. Not with a bullet hole in the bloody thing's head. At least he could walk normally now and not worry about tripping over his own feet.

He slung the costume's shoes into the gutter and stood up just as squealing tyres cut the late summer air. Good. Something bad was happening to someone else for a change. He homed in on the sounds. Some stupid moron had run out into fast moving traffic and was the new designer radiator ornament on the front of a doctor's car. He knew he shouldn't be glad, but he couldn't help it. It wasn't him this time, and at least the idiot didn't have far to go for medical help.

A song he hadn't heard in years blasted from the jukebox as he stepped into the bar. Ant Music? That was going back.

He'd barely tasted the first scotch. Or the fourth. He looked around at the costumed revellers having a fun-packed evening. They were drinking, laughing, and telling jokes. Some would probably be having sex later, but whatever they had planned, they were enjoying themselves. If he didn't track down that bag, all he had to look forward to was an overdue credit card bill, a repossession notice for his house and blackmail by a bloody kid.

He downed his fifth drink and considered his options. The gunshots had happened in the town square, and the police hadn't come which was typical. That meant going out the front was not a workable plan. At least the pub actually had a back entrance. If he went that way, he could continue searching for the second highwayman and his three million with less chance of being shot at.

The clear evening air washed over his overheated face as he stepped out onto the pavement. He closed his eyes and allowed the alcohol to spin his senses. Taking a step forwards, he stopped suddenly. He'd walked into someone, and he hoped that someone wasn't armed. The way his luck was panning out tonight, though, he wouldn't be entirely surprised if they were.

'Oi, watch where you're... Rolph?'
He knew that voice. That was the voice that spoke up at the reading of his father's will. That was the voice that belonged to the person who had stolen his inheritance. He was going to reply with a smart answer along the lines of *who were you expecting, Donkeyman?* Then he remembered the bodysuit and cape he was still wearing.

He opened his eyes, and the anger that ripped through him spun his head more than the alcohol. 'You fucking owe me.' Maybe it was the booze, but the turbo-charged blast of undiluted hatred pushed his scotch-soaked system to a whole new level of rage. The sentence his mind formed was *you're going to die,* but all his mouth could manage was 'die!'

CHAPTER 19

Ralph

Ralph's head tick-tocked between the accident and Lemmy. The Falcon Hall caretaker was splayed, possibly dead, across a car's bonnet and Yanko's eldest wasn't the slightest bit interested. His eyes and gun had laser guided missile lock and Ralph was sure it would take something properly hardcore for him to take his finger off the hot button.

Harley, however, found the pile-up fascinating and hilarious in equal measure.

'Did. You. See?' He grinned, showing a row of golden teeth. If Ralph could get Lemmy to look over at the crash, even for a second, he'd be able to dart through the stalled traffic and get out of sight by nipping up the road behind The Swan. After that he'd have to wing it, but even so, he'd have a head start.

'Harley, ya f-f-fecking h-halfwit!' Lemmy's eyes

flicked to his brother. This was his chance. It wasn't much, but it was all he had.

He sidestepped to put himself out of Lemmy's peripheral vision before launching himself into the tangle of twisted metal, broken glass and swearing motorists.

Steaming antifreeze and hot oil mingled in a garage workshop eau de cologne, with a bass note of burnt rubber, and a heady top note of spilt petrol.

He'd made it across the first lane without being shot at. Make it through the moving traffic in the other lane without ending up under it, and he could put some proper distance between him and the Un-Righteous Brothers.

'Harley!' Lemmy had spotted him. 'Stop arsing about and get after the f- fecker!'

If Lemmy hadn't loosed a bullet yet, that could only mean he hadn't got a clean shot. All he had to do, then, was keep moving.

He only had one real foot, but adrenaline did wonders for his track times. If he could keep up the pace for a few more seconds he'd reach The Swan's rear entrance. He could dive into the pub and lose himself amongst the carnival goers. Either that or hide in the bog.

He'd lost the Biddles for now, but he didn't have time to hang about outside. Standing by the pub's doorway, though, and swaying, was a worse-for-wear party animal. Animal was a good description because he was wearing a Donkeyman outfit minus the head and hooves. He was also covered in dried blood. He looked like he'd been shot, the bullet just grazing his scalp. It may have been make-up, but he didn't think so. Why dress as Donkeyman only to do yourself up as a gunshot victim?

As he neared the entrance, he could see the man had his eyes shut, and he looked terrible. Ralph stepped around him, and just as he reached for the door handle the man, eyes still firmly shut, took a step forwards nearly knocking him into a stack of beer kegs. 'Oi, watch where you're...' Now that he was up close, Ralph's recognition circuits fired all at once. He hadn't seen him since the reading of Uncle Ranulph's will. 'Rolph?'

The man's eyes flicked open and Ralph saw them focus into a beam of pure hatred.

'You fucking owe me.' His cousin, who he'd effectively stolen three million from, had stopped swaying.

'Die.' There were no grey areas, nothing to misunderstand. Rolph wanted him dead.

'Die?' Rolph may have been full of furious anger, but that only stoked Ralph's indignance. 'What, for a typo?'

'Yes, for a fucking typo! You knew that money was mine, and I bloody nearly got it all back tonight. With interest!' The unhinged anger seemed to drain away leaving a pathetic, blood caked relative.

'What money? What interest?' Ralph had a

vague idea what his cousin was gabbling on about, but he still needed it laid out for him.

Rolph shook his head and coughed out a dry laugh. 'What money? I'll tell you what money, you gullible thick shit-for-brains.' His glazed piss-head stare sharpened instantly, and with un-slurred clarity, he almost spat the words out. 'My new name is Eric Williams, and I'm Midascatman1.'

Seconds earlier his cousin wanted him dead, but those words hit Ralph harder than any fist could.

'Y-you're Midascatman1?' Seeing may have been believing, but that didn't mean his brain was ready to accept it.

Rolph, or Eric, or whatever his dumb-arse relative was calling himself nodded. 'The sodding money was nearly mine until some kid in a highwayman's outfit stole it.'

'That's no bloody kid!' If what his cousin told him was true, then all the shit that went down tonight was down to... 'That's the domesticated midas cat. That bleeding cat that you sold to me has got your cash. Get me my midas cat, and I'll get you your three million.'

'Cat?' Rolph/Eric laughed again. 'What fucking cat?' He stared skywards, and after a long moment said something that left Ralph unable to string a coherent thought together. 'There *is* no domesticated midas cat. I've been in touch with Lauren, and she told me about your obsession. I invented the whole damned thing just to get my inheritance money. Jesus, you're so fucking thick. No wonder you became a banker.'

All the tumblers in Ralph's brain lined up and dropped into place. There was no domesticated midas cat, but he had seen a midas cat. Hell, he was probably the world authority on the frigging thing. That meant it wasn't *a* midas cat, it was *the* midas cat. A cat worth the national gross domestic product was strolling around Falconbourne with three million in cash in its duffel bag.

His brain did its thing, bringing him to a conclusion that could save his life. Catch the cat and give it to the Biddles as a peace offering. Their dad's money back plus a hundred million in collateral could just get him off their murder register.

Rolph/Eric was staring hard at him and his expression told him everything he needed to know. Rolph/Eric had read him. The fucker knew. He knew there was a furry fortune out there oblivious to the fact that it was being hunted. He had to get to it before his cousin. Feigning left, he darted right, only to feel a shoulder slam into the small of his back. The bastard had rugby tackled him!

His head slammed into the aluminium beer kegs, sending them bouncing noisily into the road. The Biddles were bound to have heard the racket. That meant if he wanted to stay alive, he had to stay conscious.

CHAPTER 20

The Cat

In the old days when people were allowed to smoke in pubs, the only thing you could smell was stale beer and fags. Nowadays, however, with nothing to mask them, the over-riding odours were farts and feet. She supposed people just got used to it, but with her sensitive olfactory glands, the only thing to dull the pong was a nice pint of hoppy real ale.

Her paw closed around the smooth glass, and she inhaled. A fruity aroma with the subtle undercurrent of burnt toffee. Nice. The frothy head tickled her whisker pads as she took a deep draw. Burping, she wiped her mouth with the back of her paw. There was a great atmosphere as almost everyone had come in fancy dress. The only problem were the sounds issuing from the wall speakers. Some forgettable boy band she'd never heard of was wailing about lost love, or some such drivel. Pulling out her sequinned purse, she ambled across to the jukebox. Dog Eat Dog or Ant Music, which one to choose? She dropped the coins into the slot and touched the screen. It would be a while before it came on, but Ant Music would be worth waiting for. In the meantime, she could top up her hip flask. OK, she wasn't likely to get quality vintage malt like her sister's, but scum-scotch would have to do in a pinch.

Swinging the duffel bag off her shoulder, she un-cinched the opening and reached inside. She should have touched a stack of cakes and lobster but didn't. Something was wrong. The food had vanished, replaced by bundles of thin, slippery plastic, roughly the size of fifty pound notes. If the food had gone, there was a high probability her hip flask had gone too. What the hell was going on?

She pulled out her paw and peered inside before closing the bag. If her eyes hadn't lied to her, and she was sure they hadn't, her holdall was now stuffed with cash. Two questions popped into her head. How did it get there, and was it real?

How it got there wasn't her concern, though. It was in her bag, and that was all that mattered. As to the question of fakeness, she wasn't going to pull out a stack of notes in public, was she?

She downed the rest of her pint and headed for the pub's rear exit just as Ant Music filled the room. It was a shame she'd miss it, but she had more important things to do.

The carpark at the back of the pub was a convenient spot for Cat to inspect the money. The streetlamps in this part of town hadn't worked in years. No doubt a victim of spending cuts and local councillors skimming funds. She was about to check out a potential fortune, though, and didn't want any nosy buggers getting an eyeful, so the darkness suited her just fine.

The money had been sorted into bundles and wrapped with elastic bands. She pulled a band from one of the bundles, and it pinged into the darkness. The notes looked genuine, but she needed more light to be absolutely sure.

Spreading the wad into a fan, she held it up to her face to get a better look. Nope, she needed to get closer to the streetlights adjacent to the pub.

As she neared the road, the pub's back door crashed open, and a man dressed in a Donkeyman costume minus the head and hooves stumbled out. For some reason, he'd covered himself in fake blood, which really didn't go with the superhero costume at all.

He'd closed his eyes and was tottering towards the road just as the bald actor came hop-limping around the corner. Maybe he was on his lunchbreak and was meeting Harley and Lemmy for a friendly pint. They'd have a lot to discuss, like the next scene they'd be doing together.

As the actor reached for the door handle, Donkeyman walked into him, virtually knocking him into the stack of beer kegs.

'Oi, watch where you're...' The actor didn't look like he was acting. That meant if Donkeyman wasn't part of the cast, a real fight could break out. Cool!

'Rolph?' The actor knew Donkeyman. That was a bloody shame. That meant less chance of superhero violence. Although judging by Donkeyman's reaction, there was a strong possibility that it could kick off regardless.

From over the top of her fan of banknotes she watched Rolph, AKA Donkeyman, fill with as powerful a rage as she'd ever seen. He *really* wanted to kill the actor.

'You fucking owe me.' Rolph's voice was low and heavy with anger. Was this a real fight, or not? It certainly looked real, but what with all the fabulous street theatre going on, it could very well be another scene being played out.

'Die,' said Rolph.

Cat stared at the two men over the top of her money-fan. This was fantastic. Whether it was acting or real was irrelevant because the whole thing was electric.

'Die?' The bald actor was standing his ground. Go on, my son. Get in there!

'What, for a typo?'

Cat frowned. If this was a new scene, it didn't make sense. What was this typo thing all about? Perhaps she'd missed a scene when she went for a pint. Never mind, it would all become clear soon enough.

'Yes,' said Rolph, 'for a fucking typo. You knew that money was mine, and I bloody nearly got it all back tonight. With interest!'

It *was* part of the show. The bald bloke had stolen a stack of cash from Rolph, and Rolph had a plan to get it back. Wicked!

'What money? What interest?' said the bald bloke.

Rolph shook his blood-caked head and laughed, although he didn't sound particularly amused. 'What money? I'll tell you, you gullible thick shit-for-brains.' He paused. It must have been for dramatic effect, because what he said next almost made Cat drop her wad. 'My new name is Eric Williams, and I'm Midascatman1.'

If she'd heard what she thought she'd heard, then Rolph wasn't Rolph, he was Eric, and he was wasn't dressed as Donkeyman, he was dressed as a midas cat. He was dressed as her.

She looked down at her own outfit then back at Rolph, AKA Eric. No matter how much she screwed her eyes up and squinted, she just couldn't see it. From every angle he looked like a headless Donkeyman who'd just been shot.

'Y-you're Midascatman1?' Surely the bald actor could see that Eric didn't look anything like a midas cat. Cat didn't get it.

Eric nodded. 'The sodding money was nearly mine until some kid in a highwayman's outfit stole it.'

This was getting properly interesting. *She* had a bag of money, but it was her own bag that was filled with food one minute and wads of fifties the next. She hadn't stolen it; it had just appeared. As for the highwayman's outfit, well, it couldn't be her because she was a cat, not a kid. The only kid dressed as a highwayman was Liam and she wouldn't put it past him to not steal a stack of cash.

'That's no bloody kid!' The bald bloke was back on the offensive. Maybe there would be a fight after all. 'That's the domesticated midas cat. That bleeding cat that you sold me has got your cash. Get me my midas cat, and I'll give you your three million.'

A *domesticated* midas cat? Midas cats hadn't been domesticated since the 20th century. Great Aunt Puss was domesticated. She'd lived with Winston Churchill disguised as a butler and written all his speeches for him. Maybe the bald actor was playing the part of Churchill. If he was, though, he wasn't very convincing. He didn't have the mannerisms *or* the voice.

'Cat?' Eric laughed again, but he didn't sound particularly happy. 'What fucking cat?' He stared up at the sky without saying anything. The dramatic pause was perfectly timed, because he delivered his next line with such pathos, it left Cat reeling.

'There is no domesticated midas cat. I've been in contact with Lauren, and she told me about your obsession, so I invented the whole damned thing just to get my inheritance money. Jesus, you're so fucking thick. No wonder you became a banker.'

The story was finally coming together. It was a tale of greed, obsession, and revenge. Cat nodded to herself. It was fantastic. Bringing a midas cat into play was inspired. She'd find out who the scriptwriter was and send him a nice letter when this was all over.

A sudden movement from the Churchill character grabbed Cat's attention. Feigning left, he attempted to nip right, but Eric was way ahead of him and executed a perfect rugby tackle. Even though Cat knew it was all play acting, she couldn't help but get swept up by the whole thing. Churchill headbutted the metal beer kegs hard enough to send them clanging into the road.

An intriguing plot, lots of action, and a midas cat. This play had to be in line for an award. Just as Cat didn't think it could get any more exciting, the two swamp dwellers she'd seen earlier re-appeared, and they looked properly murderous.

'R-R-Ralph!' It was Lemmy, Cat's favourite. He'd pulled out his replica pistol again. This time she had a better view of it, and it looked as though it could really kill someone. Impressive.

'What the fuck's going on?' said Eric. 'Who the hell are you?'

'None. Of. Your. Business.' Harley fought to get the words out which heightened the thrill level.

Eric took a step towards the swamp brothers and stopped when Lemmy raised the gun.

'D-don't you f-f-fucking m-m-move!' Eric raised his hands, palms out, just like a western movie. The play must have been nearing its climax. The tension was so great, Cat could almost taste it. Although, to be fair, it may just have been the kitchen sink burger repeating on her.

'R-R-Ralph!' Lemmy's shout made the Churchill character flinch.

'G-get up sl-slowly.'

'OK, Lemmy. Anything you say, mate.'

'D-don't call me mate, y-ya m-murdering piece of sh-shit!'

Ralph pulled himself upright by hanging onto the last vertical beer keg.

'Ralph,' said Eric. 'Who *are* these blokes, and what do they want?'

'If you want to live, shut the fuck up!' Ralph was trying to calm Eric, and the excitement had reached such a high, Cat didn't think she could take much more. She didn't want to stay, but she didn't want to leave, either. It was like watching a horror movie from behind the sofa. That's when an idea flashed through her mind. She could stay and watch, but she didn't have to listen. If she fired up her iPod, she could catch all the action without the words.

Adam Ant's Puss in Boots filled her head with stereo perfection, giving her an uncontrollable urge to dance. She threw a paw into the air. 'Bugger!' She'd forgotten about her fistful of cash. Fifty-pound notes fluttered to the ground, covering the pavement with expensive confetti. If she didn't pick it up immediately, however, she'd probably forget all about it.

She straightened up just as Harley's face went blank. Or, at least, blanker than usual. He had a small feathered dart imbedded in his forehead and just before his fingers touched it, he collapsed, faceplanting a metal barrel. This was a new development. A sniper firing drug-bullets at the swamp people. Cool!

If she moved a bit to her left, she'd get a better view and catch more of the action. She scooted over just as a shot sparked off a keg near Ralph's right leg. They hadn't skimped on the special effects. This was every bit as good as a Hollywood blockbuster.

Lemmy grabbed Ralph around the neck and pressed the pistol into his temple just as headlamps flooded the street with blue-white light. A bunch of hard looking blokes piled out of five cars, and they were seriously tooled up with pump action shotguns, automatic pistols and revolvers. Whoever this lot were, they were up for a fight. This was absolutely amazing. The Sweeney and Lemmy were now in a Mexican stand-off with Ralph and Eric being held as hostages. How was this going to end?

CHAPTER 21

Jeffrey

He must have blacked out. He was chasing the cat through the traffic, and then bang! How long had he been out for?

'Don't attempt to move until I examine you.' Someone was shining a torch in his eyes. 'It's OK, I'm a doctor.'

So was he, and he was a bloody good one. Falcon Hall couldn't function without him. 'I'm all right.' At least, he hoped he was. Nothing screamed *broken bones,* just a few bodily twinges moaned *bruises, scrapes, and a bump on the head.*

'Let me be the judge of that.' The doctor may have meant well, but he was holding him up. The longer he lay in a puddle of antifreeze, the further away his talking cat was getting. 'I'm also a doctor. I work at Falcon Hall.'

'I know all the medical staff at that facility. I don't remember you.'

Jeffrey didn't have time for a chit-chat, even if it was with a fellow professional. 'I've got work to do.' The whack to his head was worse than he first thought because when he staggered to his feet, the steady throb turned to a heavy metal bass drumbeat.

'You must allow me to examine you. You may need an ambulance.' Doctor Do-Gooder was starting to annoy him.

'Fuck off and leave me alone. You're the one that ran me over in the first place.' Doctor Do-Gooder took a step back giving Jeffrey enough space to plan his escape.

The traffic in the far lane was, unfortunately, moving. If he waited until it stopped, he could wait all bloody night, so without over-thinking it, he nipped out. Horns blared, but what did it matter? He was safely across...this time. Now all he had to do was locate the creature that was going to make his fortune.

Did the cat follow the road that ran behind the pub? If it did, it could either continue on to Midland Park or enter the pub. If it did neither, then he wouldn't know where to start the search. What would the cat do? What would *he* do? Well, if it was a choice between going on the swings or having a pint, it was pretty bloody obvious.

Raised voices came from the pub's rear entrance. A fight was about to break out, and if he got involved in any way, even as a police witness, it could hold him up for hours. He needed to stick to the shadows, and the carpark opposite was perfect. Once the drunken idiots had finished with each other, he'd be able to pop into The Swan for a look around.

Hunkering down behind a rust speckled Ford, he focused on the argument. Two tramp-like characters had another two men at gunpoint. This was more than your usual drunken punch up. The man in the Donkeyman outfit had already been shot, and Jeffrey recognised the other man as Ralph Williams. Luckily, none of the four could see the cat as they were all facing the wrong way.

The tricorne hat, boots and coat were unmistakable, as were the whiskers sticking out either side of the fan of fifty pound notes. What to do? If he shot the cat, the sudden movement of it collapsing would attract attention. He had to do something, though, and quick.

'Ralph,' said Donkeyman. 'Who *are* these blokes, and what do they want?'

It didn't matter to Jeffrey who they were. He just wished they'd go and kill each other somewhere else. Then he could get on with the job of capturing his midas cat.

'If you want to live,' said Ralph, 'shut the fuck up!'

It didn't look like anybody was going anywhere, so he just had to take a chance and shoot the cat.

He leaned across the old car's bonnet and steadied the pistol. One shot should do it. Resting his head on his hand, he stared down the barrel. What was the stupid animal doing? It was fiddling about with a phone, or something. Oh no! The loopy feline had started dancing. He now had a moving target. 'Bloody well stand still,' he muttered to himself.

The *phut* of the air-powered weapon was almost silent, but the cat seemed to have heard it, nonetheless. It bent at the waist and the dart whirred over its head hitting the shorter of the two tramps. He'd missed the target, but at least he'd put one of the men out of action.

A bell-like clang rang out as the man landed face first on a metal beer keg. The pistol only took one dart at a time, and it wouldn't take anyone long to figure out where the shots came from. He had to re-load and finish this.

Steadying the pistol once again, he lined up the sights. Not again! The bastard animal sidestepped the dart and it sparked harmlessly off a keg. Jesus! What did he have to use to catch the damned thing, a machine gun?

The suited tramp grabbed Ralph and jammed the gun barrel into his temple just as the road filled with growling, screeching cars. The hardest armed men Jeffrey had ever seen poured into the street.

He was wielding a single shot drug air pistol, and they were brandishing shotguns and hand cannons. If they spotted him pointing it in their direction, he'd end up with more perforations than a teabag. What to do? Nobody had spotted him or the cat yet, but it was only a matter of time.

'You in the suit. Put the fucking gun down!' The lead hard man pointed a pump action twelve bore at Ralph and the tramp. If he pulled the trigger, he'd vaporise Ralph, the tramp *and* Donkeyman. 'Rolph, is that you?' The hard man knew one of the men?

'Frank, get me out of here!' Donkeyman was heading towards a fear fuelled melt-down. If he panicked, there'd be a shootout and the talking cat could get killed in the crossfire.

'Somebody call the cops!' Ralph had manned up. Although, given his current situation, it was an incredibly stupid thing to do.

'We *are* the cops!' Frank didn't fill Jeffrey with a whole load of confidence.

'Rolph,' said Frank. 'I'll get you out of here, but when I do, we're going to have a little chat about you and Liam.' Rolph AKA Donkeyman's already terror-filled face took on a whole new level of dread. By the looks of things, he'd have been better off facing the armed vagrants alone.

'You in the scarecrow suit, I won't tell you again. Drop the weapon!'
If Jeffrey didn't do it immediately, there was a chance he never would. He re-loaded and took aim.

'The midas cat!' Ralph had seen the cat. This was un-good. 'The midas cat. It's there by the lamp post!'

Jeffrey pulled the trigger. Oh shit, he'd shot a cop. One of the undercover boys slumped to the ground. Not only was that a guaranteed prison sentence, it would probably start a wild west shoot out with the cat in the firing line.

'Spader, what just happened?' said Frank.

'Dunno, Chief.' Spader bent to inspect the downed cop. He'd find the dart stuck in his colleague's neck and eventually trace it back. Jeffrey was beyond fucked, but if he could get the cat and escape, he could make enough money to travel the world, and they'd never catch him.

'Which one of you arseholes just shot my DI?' Thankfully, Frank was as thick as pig shit and hadn't figured it out, because jigging about less than ten feet away was a priceless talking cat.

'The midas cat!' Ralph had either not heard or chose to ignore Frank's outburst. 'Lemmy, you have to believe me. Standing just over there is a mega-rare animal, and it killed your dad. It's also worth one hundred million.' Ralph was almost screaming now. 'It's got your dad's three million in its backpack. Take it,' he screeched. 'Peace offering. Just don't kill me.'

Lemmy stared past the cops. He'd seen it too. 'Feck, it's a cat dressed as a highwayman!'

'What the hell have you two been taking?' There was a ker-chunk as Frank chambered a round.

'Oh shit. Frank, behind you!' Donkeyman had joined in. 'It's real. The bloody midas cat is real!'

'Oh for fuck's sake,' said Frank 'Don't you bloody

start.' The other cops raised their weapons as the tramp pointed his gun across at the cat.

'Look, it's...' The tramp never finished his sentence. The shotgun blast echoed off the pub wall. If Jeffrey hadn't seen Ralph lose it with his own eyes, he could easily have mistaken the screaming for a six-year-old girl's.

The top of Lemmy's head had come off, splattering Donkeyman and Ralph in lumpy red semolina. That was the best distraction he was ever likely to get, so he reached into his pocket for the final dart, but all his fingers found was a boiled sweet and an old tissue.

'Jeffrey!' He knew that voice. 'Jeffrey, there you are. I've been searching all over town for you.' It was the voice of childhood misery. He ignored it and watched the cat adjust the driver's seat of one of the un-marked police cars.

'Jeffrey, if you ignore me, you know what will happen.' Oh, he knew all right. It was impossible, though. Mother was bed-bound. It couldn't be her.

Just as the midas cat drove away, he turned to face the voice.

'I found this under the fridge.' He wasn't sure if it was the Tupperware box and the memories of week old roast that made him feel sick, or the maggot-ridden rat writhing about inside it. Jesus! Had she been wandering about town with that thing on display?

'Y-you're bed-bound,' he stuttered.

'No I'm not, stupid boy. I've been faking it in

order to keep tabs on you, and it looks like I was right to do so.'

The screaming had stopped, but he no longer cared. He'd lost his chance of fame and a matching bank balance. It was over.

'Home!' Mother was winding up the lecture machine. 'Now!' As if he had a choice.

CHAPTER 22

Eric, The Conman Previously Known As Rolph

Eric looked towards the heavens. Hadn't his cousin figured it out yet? 'There is no domesticated midas cat. I've been in contact with Lauren, and she told me about your obsession, so I invented the whole damned thing just to get my inheritance money. Jesus, you're so fucking thick. No wonder you became a banker.'

He'd been pissed and on his way to plastered only seconds ago, but now he was soberer than he'd felt in a while. If he stared Ralph down, could he get him to give him his money back? As he lasered a killer look into Ralph's eyes, he saw it. Ralph had something figured out but what? The midas cat was Ralph's obsession. Yes, he knew that. Ralph's expression was one of eureka. Obsession, midas cat. Midas cat, obsession. He moved the pieces around in his head. Obsession, midas cat, eureka. The final piece completed the picture. The kid in the highwayman's outfit that wasn't Liam was a real midas cat, and it was worth a skipful of money.

Ralph knew that he knew. He broke left, but Eric had him cold. As he hustled right, Eric hit him low and hard, bringing him down headfirst into the beer kegs with a chiming clang.

'R-R-Ralph!' Eric leapt to his feet in time to see a couple of what he assumed to be homeless guys. The one in the scabby pinstripe suit had pulled a gun. He didn't know much about pistols, but what *was* there to know apart from not being on the wrong end when it went off.

'What the fuck's going on?' He said that more to himself than anything. 'Who the hell are you?' It probably wasn't a good idea asking a psychotic armed vagrant stupid questions, but he couldn't help himself.

'None. Of. Your. Business.' The second of the two didn't just look dangerous, he looked and sounded deranged. Whatever this was, it had nothing to do with him. If Ralph was being hunted by a pair of nutters, that was his business. It was time to go. He took a step forwards.

'D-don't you f-fucking m-m-move!' Pinstripe raised the gun, and Eric raised his hands. Rule number one: Always do what the gunman says.

'R-Ralph!' Out of the corner of his eye, Eric was sure he saw his cousin flinch.

'G-get up. Sl-slowly.'

'OK, Lemmy. Anything you say, mate.' Did Ralph really call the loopy fucker *mate*?

'D-don't call me m-m-mate, y-ya m-murdering piece of sh-shit!'

Had he imagined it, or had Ralph just been called a murderer? What the hell had he done?

Ralph dragged himself upright.

'Ralph, who are these blokes, and what do they want?' He already had a pretty good idea but needed clarification. Yes, his cousin had killed someone but who and how? And what did this pair of lowlifes have to do with it all?

'If you want to live, shut the fuck up!' There was a definite tremble to Ralph's voice that wasn't faked. This shit, whatever this shit was, was real.

A barely audible *phut* he wouldn't normally have noticed came from the carpark opposite. In his heightened state of awareness, however, the slightest sound registered as a possible threat. He would have dismissed it if the shorter of the two men hadn't face-planted one of the beer kegs. Somebody was shooting at them with a silenced weapon. Christ, this was spy movie territory, not real life. Only, it was real life, wasn't it!

That's when everything happened at once. Headlights from at least four cars locked onto the three of them, the pinstriped pikey grabbed Ralph around the neck, and a gang of armed skinheads surrounded them.

'You in the suit,' said the lead skinhead. 'Put the

fucking gun down!' Eric couldn't be sure due to the blinding headlights, but wasn't the lead-man Frank Stone, his next door neighbour?

'Rolph, is that you?'

Yes, it *was* Frank. He was saved. OK, so Frank didn't know his new-and-improved name yet, but that didn't really matter. 'Frank, get me out of here!'

'Somebody call the cops!' Ralph's voice drifted into his consciousness. The idiot hadn't realised, had he?

'We *are* the fucking cops!' shouted Frank. 'I won't tell you again.' Frank's shotgun pointed at Ralph and armed suit-man. 'Put down the fucking gun!'

Why didn't Frank get him out of there? Was he enjoying it? That was it, wasn't it. This was payback for getting caught dressing Liam as a midas cat. He looked from Frank to Ralph and pulled up short. Ralph wasn't focussed on the gang of police but on something in the middle distance, and he had the faintest of smiles. What the hell did he have to smile about? He only had minutes to live.

'The midas cat!' Ralph's blurt raised more weapons and, no doubt, tightened fingers on triggers. What was he planning, suicide by cop?

'The midas cat,' he said again. 'It's there by the lamp post!'

There was that *phut* again. It was on the edge of his hearing, but it was there. One of the policemen slumped lifeless to the ground. Oh shit! A dead cop meant Frank and Co would open fire thinking

Lemmy had done it. They were gagging for a fight; he could almost smell it.

Even though he knew he'd probably be dead in a few seconds, he couldn't resist following Ralph's gaze. Liam? The highwayman's outfit was the first thing he saw, followed by a pair of glassy green eyes shining from a tabby and white furry face. He'd made it all up, so how comes it was bopping about on the far side of the road?

'The midas cat!' Ralph's voice had notched up an octave. The stupid moron was being held captive by an armed pikey, was in the middle of a standoff with Frank and the boys and was screeching about a talking cat.

'That's who killed your dad,' said Ralph. 'It's worth a hundred million, and it's got your dad's three million in its backpack. Take it!' He must have been talking to his captor whose father was killed by the midas cat. 'Take it!' he yelled. 'Peace offering. Please, Lemmy. Don't kill me.'

Lemmy's head moved ever so slightly. 'Feck, it's a cat dressed as a highwayman!'

'What the hell are you two on?' Frank pumped the shotgun, chambering a shell. If he didn't get Frank to look round at the mythical talking cat who was, apparently, the root cause of all this, he was likely to end up crapping out of an extra hole. 'Frank, behind you!' He knew it was, to quote the cliché, the oldest trick in the book, but he wasn't messing. This wasn't a trick. 'It's real. The bloody midas cat is real!'

'Don't *you* start.' Frank wasn't going to turn around, and neither were any of his team. The cat, the sniper, they didn't exist. It was just Ralph, Lemmy and him.

That was not the best moment for Lemmy to spring a catastrophic stupidity leak. He pointed his gun across the road. In hindsight, Eric knew what he was doing. He was pointing at the midas cat, using the pistol like a finger. If he'd have dropped the damned thing first, he wouldn't have had the top of his head non-surgically removed.

The screaming that pierced the ringing in his ears following the shotgun blast was too close to be anything other than either himself or Ralph. Before he had a chance to analyse it, cold steel cut into his wrists.

'I don't know what you're mixed up in, Rolph, but the pair of you are coming with me.'

He was going to prison for fraud. Frank didn't know that yet, but he soon would. The thing was, he'd make damned sure his thieving cousin went down with him. He didn't know how just yet, but he'd figure something out.

CHAPTER 23

The Cat

Cat stared at the scene playing out in front of her and wondered why she was the only one watching. Skinheads with shotguns, an unconscious swamp person with a drug dart sticking out of his forehead, a hostage situation... Where was the rest of the audience? This was brilliant. There was shouting and gesturing, and all to the soundtrack of Adam Ant's *Puss in Boots.*

With the music playing, it was almost balletic. Was balletic a real word? She was sure she'd heard Yolanda mention it a few times. If the professor used it, it must be a real word. Real or not, the moves performed by the actors flowed in perfect time to the track on her iPod which gave her an itch to join in. She knew she mustn't, though, because that would shatter the illusion of reality. She could dance along from her spot by the lamp post, though.

The moment she threw a particularly funky shape, one of the hard men collapsed just as Ralph started jigging in Lemmy's grip. With the music, it was like a street version of the Les Mis musical Yolanda had taken her to see.

Ralph was staring straight at her. It was almost as if she was part of the play. This was totally immersive stuff. When Lemmy pointed his gun at her, she let out an involuntary shiver. Knowing the pistol wasn't real didn't lessen the impact of having someone point a weapon at you, though. Getting a scare from a good horror movie was exciting, sure, but this was a whole new level of thrilling.

Lemmy had gone into one, eyes bugging out as if he was on drugs, followed immediately by Rolph, or as he was now calling himself, Eric. What had happened? Was there some sort of panic virus going through them?

The three men's urgent, jerky movements ceased the second fire spat from the lead skinhead's shotgun. How they did it was way clever. Lemmy's head exploded, splattering Eric and Ralph with fake brains and bits of skull. In a Hollywood blockbuster it would have been done using computers, but this was a live show. It looked as though the top of Lemmy's head had been blown clean off. Fantastic!

The screaming was so loud, it cut through Adam Ant. Not to worry, though. The play must have been ending because the skinhead had handcuffed Ralph and Eric. The hard men must have been plainclothes police, like the Sweeney. That made Ralph and Eric criminals. Now she'd seen the whole play, it all made perfect sense. Ralph and Eric had stolen the three million quid from the swamp people, and the sniper was after the cash, but the police got there first. That made the money in her duffel bag a worthless prop. Not to worry, though. She'd keep it anyway, as a souvenir.

Now the play was over, there wasn't much point hanging around. Besides, she had an appointment to keep in Cambridge. She needed transport, though, as taking the bus with a bunch of poor people and piss-heads was not an option. Over the road, however, was a nice collection of un-marked police cars. She knew they were only movie props, but they were still real cars. The producer wouldn't mind if she borrowed one for the night. The play *was* over and so was carnival week, so they wouldn't be needed for a while.

After adjusting the driving seat, Cat got behind the wheel of the rearmost car. It was dead authentic inside with an eye for detail that was so good, she could almost have sworn it was the genuine article. It had a police-band radio, switches for the blue lights and sirens, and it even had a replica automatic pistol in the glove compartment. The producer had thought of everything.

The university's wood panelled corridor smelled of lemon polish and wax with an undercurrent of sour acid, rotten eggs and gunpowder smoke. Cat raised a paw.

'Come in.' Yolanda knew she was there, even though Cat hadn't had a chance to knock on her office door.

'Hi, Yoda.' Yolanda looked up from the antique Bakelite radio she was fiddling with and shot Cat a look that said *if you call me that again, I'll conduct a painful experiment on you.*

'Sit down and be quiet.' Yolanda wound the brass tuning dial until Big Ben's chimes rang out. 'The midnight news is about to start.'

'Here is the news from the BBC.' The second bong vibrated the vintage wireless. 'A gunfight in a Hertfordshire town has left one dead and two wounded. Three men have been taken into custody and are helping police with their enquiries.'

'That's nothing,' said Cat and switched the radio off. 'I've just seen a really cool bit of street theatre.'

'Oh yeah?' Cat's brother Jimmy peeled himself out of the leather armchair by the crackling fire and yawned widely.

'Yeah,' said Cat. 'There was this gunfight. One bloke got killed and two got wounded. It was brilliant.' She upended the duffel bag onto the professor's desk. 'Oh, and I found this.' Bundles of banknotes tumbled over the edge onto the floor. 'There should be three million, give or take.' She smiled. 'Get the monopoly board out.'

PART 2: JOURNEY TO THE CENTRE OF THE CAT

CHAPTER 1

Ralph

Ralph stared at his reflection in the bathroom mirror. The boils hadn't gone. They had, if anything, got worse. He shook his head, and the extra pepperoni with anchovies also shook its head.

If he hadn't caved into his wife's demands for a midas cat, he wouldn't be divorced, on the run from the police for suspected murder and testing germ warfare antidotes in a secretive police state, would he? All this shit because of a talking cat!

He'd done the business...almost. When he'd found a midas cat online and borrowed three million from *The Cash flow King*, Yanko Biddle, in order to pay for it, he'd honestly thought he'd win Lauren back. Yeah, right!

The incident involving the cat, a Range Rover, a caravan, and an unfinished flyover was a nasty way for old man Biddle to die. Maybe he shouldn't have chosen that exact moment to use the caravan's toilet?

After the accident, he'd skipped bail and escaped to North Katistonia. It was the only place, apart from the moon, where Frank Stone and his legalised gang of thugs, AKA The Flying Squad, wouldn't think of looking for him. Unfortunately, *Our Glorious Leader*, Kang Dog Wang, pegged him for a spy and had given him a choice: Work in a chemical weapons lab road-testing new recipes, or spend fifty years turning great big rocks into little tiny rocks with nothing but a toffee hammer.

He shuffled back into the living room and switched on the TV. He couldn't understand a word of it, but it didn't matter because there were only two programmes. He could either watch the rolling political broadcast by the Katistonian People's Party on Channel One or the news on Channel Two, both of which told him nothing other than how great President Kang was. He opted for the news.

'Kang Dog Wang... blah, blah... President Manx... blah, blah...'

Ralph's head shot up. US President, Marcus L Manx, had spent billions on a winter sports complex just north of the Mexican border in order to strengthen ties with *Our Friends in the South.* Mexicans had as much use for skeleton bobsleighs as the Dutch had for mountaineering boots, so what was that idiot up to now? Crude graphics trundled across the screen followed by photos of Kang and The Leader of the Free World. From what he could make out, Manx was on a state visit to discuss de-militarisation. There was also a peace envoy from the world's most prestigious universities. Professors from Harvard, Yale, Oxford, Cambridge, and a whole load more he'd never heard of would be attending. As if that would do any bloody good!

He turned off the TV just as the phone rang. He knew who it was before he even picked it up. Nobody else ever called him. He lifted the receiver. He had to answer because it was illegal not to.

'Walph.' It was Quock. It couldn't be anyone else because he was the only one who could speak English.

'You work. Now!' At nine o'clock? What did that imperious little shit want at this time of night?

Ralph blinked in the harsh glare of the defence development building. Half built rockets sat in cradles next to huge metal drums of weapons-grade plutonium. That had scared the dinner out of him for the first few weeks, but now it was just part of everyday life.

'All right, Quock, what's shaking, dude?' He loved using western slang because nobody could understand a word. He'd even tried a few swear words just to see what he could get away with. *Shit-head* and *arsehole* didn't register, so for three weeks he'd greeted everyone as either Mr Shithead or Mr Arsehole. When Quock asked him what it meant, he'd told him it was slang for intelligent and good looking.

It went viral. In the dining hall he'd overhear unintelligible conversations with the occasional *shit-head* thrown in. His favourite, though, was when Quock tried to chat up the dinner lady. He'd leant on the counter, lit up an untipped, winked at her, and in his smoothest delivery blurted out *arsehole.* Ralph nearly lost his lunch and had to feign a coughing fit.

'Walph!' Quock glared up at him. 'You listen!'

As if he had a choice.

'You good worker. You chosen. It great honour. Dangerous mission. You spy on West.'

Spy? On the West? He was going home. Get back and go straight to the pub. Then Mc Donald's... then the pub again. Then maybe he'd go to the authorities.

'Me inject you.' Quock held a cattle-sized syringe filled with a cloudy green liquid. Before Ralph had a chance to complain, Quock had plunged the needle into his thigh.

'Ow, fuck! You arsehole!'

'Thank you, Walph. You very kind. Anyway, me explain. This L E G zero. Top secret. Me give you further instructions when you inside inner spacecraft.'

Inner spacecraft? What was the plank talking about? His head spun, and his vision blurred. He'd been so pumped up on toxic weaponry, he was surprised anything could have an effect on him.

The last thing he saw was Quock's grinning face, and then everything went black.

Ralph's eyes shot open. He'd been injected with God-knows-what. He tried to stand but couldn't. He was strapped to a chair. What were they doing this time, electrocuting him? As his vision cleared, a 1950s East German-style dashboard and steering wheel came into view. Where the sun visors should have been, there was a vast array of switches, lights and buttons. Had Quock drugged him just to make him drive a Cold War era *car-of-the-future?*

'Walph.' He looked around to see where the voice came from. 'Walph. Pick up microphone.'
A tinny Quock rattled from a loudspeaker in a radio set that had probably been built in the sixties.

'Err, what?'

'Look out windscreen.'
He did. Through a bubbly haze he could see a roomful of people. It was some sort of posh do.

'Controls like car,' said Quock. 'Steers like plane.'
Ralph hit the accelerator, spun the craft around and saw a familiar face. The shiny black fur and huge green eyes had looked out of every TV news report for over a week. The problem, though, was the scale. Either that face was enormous, or... Realisation hit him hard. He'd been shrunk to miniscule size and was in a tiny submarine floating in

a glass of champagne. Things were about to get a whole lot worse, though, because in a few seconds the midas cat's sister, the only feline Cambridge professor in history, was going to swallow him.

CHAPTER 2

The Cat

Cat stared at the sign. There was something wrong with it. It should have read *Welcome to South Katistonia,* followed by some blurb about the annual winter games. Instead it read *All Hail Our Glorious Leader* in fifteen different languages.

Pictures of a fat schoolboy with an insane pudding-basin haircut were everywhere. The kid was either wanted by the police or had gone missing. Still, if Cat was forced to have a hair-do as stupid as that, she'd want to run away from her evil parents as well. Poor bloody kid.

She pulled back the sleeve of her tabby fake-fur coat and glanced at her watch for the twentieth time. She tapped it. Had it broken or had time stopped? She'd been in the queue for at least a day, but her watch told her it had only been an hour. *Only* an hour? What were those Mickey Mouse numpties up to? She was here for the winter games and at the rate she was going, they'd be over before she'd even cleared duty free. Which reminded her. Where *was* duty free? No shops, no bars, no adverts. Once she'd thought about it, she realised there wasn't much of anything, only dozens of pictures of the fat kid. When she'd cleared passport control, though, everything would be fine.

Cat looked around the grey room. The uniformed bozos had dragged her out of the queue and hustled her through a door. Why they insisted on speaking to her in Katistonian, she had no idea. It meant sod all to her. That had been hours ago, though, and she was now hungry. She'd been left for so long; they'd probably forgotten about her. She tried the door. Locked. She shrugged and stuck a claw into the keyhole.

The hallway beyond the door was every bit as grey as the room, but at least it was empty. Pulling on her coat, she strode towards what she hoped was the exit, slammed a paw down on the crash bar and stepped out onto the night-time street as a siren cut through the frosty air. It was probably that fat kid causing trouble. No wonder there were wanted posters of him everywhere. That, however, was somebody else's problem because her priority, right now, was finding food and up ahead was the answer.

The palace had moonlit snow-dusted onion domes and was enormous. Any place that big was bound to have a restaurant, and a kitchen. The armed guards around the entrance didn't look friendly, though, but she'd find a way in. She always did.

CHAPTER 3

The Professor

It had been a great year for Professor Yolanda Barnes. Not only had she made history by becoming the first cat to earn a place at Cambridge, she'd been invited to North Katistonia as part of the International Scholars' Peace Envoy.

She looked around the palace ballroom at her fellow academics and smiled. It felt good to be part of something great.

President Manx was meeting Kang Dog Wang in public for the first time ever, and she was here to witness it in person. It was a good time to be alive, and her daft tabby sister wasn't here to ruin it for her. She nodded to herself. Cat had gone to the annual winter games in South Katistonia which would keep her busy for at least a week, so no worries on that score.

'You want champagne?'

The professor looked up. The Katistonian waiter

bore a silver tray with a lone glass at its centre. She'd been singled out for special treatment, as nobody else on her table had been offered any. They must know how important she was. 'Thank you.'

The condensation from the icy cold glass damped her fur as she gripped the flute. She inhaled. Fruity with a hint of vanilla and apple blossom made it either a sixty four or five. Either way, it was a good vintage.

'Very good, madam.' The waiter melted back into the crowd, and Yolanda held the glass up to the light. She squinted at the wine and frowned. 'That's just typical,' she muttered to herself. 'Corked!' A tiny speck bobbed about amongst the bubbles. She had a good mind to complain but seeing as she'd been invited, she decided against it.

'May I have your attention, please?' The Master of Ceremonies stood on the balcony above the dance floor. 'Our Glorious Leader has asked me to thank you all for attending this momentous occasion. Please raise your glasses for a toast. To peace and friendship.'

Everybody stood and raised their glasses. 'Peace and friendship.' She took a deep swallow, and the bubbles tickled her nose.

As she took her seat again, the room blurred for a second. Something wasn't right. She shook her head as the background chatter increased to unbearable levels, the light drilled into her retinas, and her head pulsed with a dull, insistent throb.

'Excuse me, would you?' She pushed back her chair. If she went for a lie down, perhaps she'd feel better in a short while.

As she stood, a blast of stomach-gas erupted from under her tail with enough power to rattle the cutlery. What the hell was in that champagne?

CHAPTER 4

Ralph

'Walph. You follow alcohol through stomach wall into bloodstream.'
'Yes, Mein Fuhrer.'
'What you say?'
'Nothing.' No rollercoaster could have prepared Ralph for the experience of jetting down a cat's digestive tract. To call it a white-knuckle ride didn't do it justice. He had the illusion of control only because he had a steering wheel, but it was as effective as a dinghy rudder on The Titanic.

Christ knows what the cat ate for breakfast, but the visibility in the stomach was less than nil. Follow the alcohol? In this soup he couldn't follow the scent of his own fart. He floored the accelerator hoping he was going the right way and felt the pull of a whirlpool from under him.

'Quock, what the fuck's going on?' A biological

bathplug had just been uncorked, and he was getting sucked into its current.

'Stomach draining into intestine. You no go that way. You do, you die.'

He was in a cat's stomach. He didn't rate his chances, anyway, but being told about it didn't make him feel any better.

He mashed his foot into the floor, but the little craft went nowhere. As hard as he pushed the sub, the vortex pulled just as hard.

Sweat popped on his forehead. If he didn't get through the stomach wall, he was dead.

'Walph. Use nitrous button.'

'You might have told me sooner, shitstick!' He slammed a palm down on the red button marked with a large *N*.

The effect was immediate. The little sub torpedoed forwards with a fiery blast.

'That'll give the sodding cat some serious wind.' Ralph chuckled to himself as he hurtled towards the stomach wall. 'Oh bugger!' He reached for the reverse thrust button.

'No press reverse thrust,' said Quock. 'Go faster.' He had no choice but to trust Quock. He wasn't dead yet, so Quock had to be doing something right. He screwed his eyes shut and braced for impact, but instead of a metal tearing crunch, there was a gentle slowing, and a quiet *plop*.

He'd done it! He'd made it into the bloodstream. Now what?

'Walph.' The speaker crackled to life. 'Well

done. Me got you on GPS. Turn next right. It go to brain.'

Ralph threw the autopilot switch and watched the red and white blood cells jockey for position. It was like watching trucks overtaking each other on the highway but far more fascinating.

'What happens now?'

'Turnoff ahead. Then you deploy reverse thrust.'

He disengaged autopilot and reached for the indicator. Who was he signalling, though? He was the only one in here.

The blood vessels in the brain were far smaller and more like back alleys compared to the six lane freeway arteries of the main body.

Reverse thrust slowed him to a gentle stop. 'Yo, Quock.' Yo. Quock will never get that one.

'Walph, my main man. How it hang?'

How it hang? Had he been studying a book of Western slang? 'I'm in the brain.'

'OK. Deploy anchor and neural interface. Computer controls on heads-up screen.'

Sure enough, all the controls were there. Walk, speak, arms and paw controls, with the screen's main part taken up with a panel marked *visuals.*

'What's it all for?'

'Hit feline over-ride button and you control cat. You in driving seat.'

As the info sunk in, Ralph's face stretched into an unfamiliar shape as he grinned for the first time in months. The sister of the cat that had caused him a world of pain was now under his complete control.

'This is going to be fun.'

'What you say?'

'I said there's work to be done.' He'd start by making the animal wear a lampshade for a hat, and then he'd just wing it. Quock had no idea what he'd done.

CHAPTER 5

The Cat

It had started snowing, and armoured cars and tanks filled the streets. Fuck knows what the ugly fat kid had done this time, but the authorities were well pissed off with him.

Cat slipped up a side street behind the palace and there they were. Industrial sized wheelie bins sat in an orderly row along the back wall near a non-descript door. Where there's bins, there's kitchens, and all Cat had to do was wait for someone to chuck something out and she'd be in. Sorted!

The steam filling the kitchens smelled divine. Soup, steak, boiled this, fried that and sautéed the other. Cat wouldn't go hungry. Or detected. Not in the food-fog, anyway.

She liberated a chop from a frying pan whilst the chef stirred the stew, freed some caviar from a shelf and broke out a lobster from its pot. No, she wasn't going to go hungry.

There was only one thing to procure now, and that was the booze. A fine dinner deserves fine wine. 'North Katistonian cooking sherry,' said Cat. 'Get in!' She popped the cork and downed the contents in one before her ears pricked up. The sound of a party drifted from beyond the kitchen door. Cat loved a good party, especially an 80s themed party. 'Hope there's some Adam Ant,' she said and pushed open the door into the ballroom.

CHAPTER 6

The Professor

She was a Cambridge professor, so why did she have an unstoppable urge to wear a lampshade as a hat?

She tore the shade from the floor lamp and checked her reflection in the mirror. She looked like a hen night reject but couldn't stop herself from laughing hysterically.

Her behaviour was out of control. More to the point, it was out of *her* control. It had all started when she'd drunk the champagne. That was it! She must have been drugged. Why, then, was everything so clear? She was totally lucid. Only, she had no control over her body.

She farted and did a paw-pump. 'Fart-tastic!' She'd never say anything so crude. That was something her sister would say. 'I am Professor Fartpelt!' Why had she said that? Things were getting worse.

She ran into the bathroom and grabbed the toilet roll from its holder. She was now armed. Which one would she hit with it, though, Manx or Kang? They were both arseholes, so it didn't matter. It would jump-start World War Three whichever one she got.

She was part of an international peace envoy, and she was planning on starting a war? She walked over to the door and rested a paw on the handle. She mustn't go out. She had to stay in her room. At least that way... Too late! Wearing an orange lantern hat and a red velvet curtain toga, she swept down the stairs before taking a deep bow.

The lampshade slipped down her forehead before bouncing all the way to the ballroom floor. She'd made a complete tit of herself but couldn't stop.

Her table was within bog-roll range of the balcony, so when *Great Leader* and *Other Great Leader* came out, she'd have a perfect shot.

She glanced around the room and stopped when the kitchen door crashed open. It was her sister, Cat! Feelings of vengeance, embarrassment and fear fought for superiority. What the hell was going on?

CHAPTER 7

Ralph

'Walph!' Quock had lost it. 'Walph! What you do?'

'Anything I fucking like!' The lampshade hat and curtain toga were pure genius. The sodding cat belonged to him, and he was having way too much fun to stop now. What with Manx and Kang due to meet up in public, it was about to get a whole lot better. Oh, God that was sweet. Get the animal stitched up for starting an international incident. Shame it wasn't the tabby one, though.

He rotated the cat through 180 degrees and scanned the room. The visuals on the computer screen showed everything the animal could see. He was looking out through its eyes.

'Right.' Ralph zoomed in on the balcony above the dancefloor. 'That's where the two leaders will shake hands. The full toilet roll should be just the right weight.'

'Walph!' Quock screamed at him. 'You need be incognito!' By the sound of it, he'd birthed his first kitten. Ralph grinned. He was going to drop a whole litter by the time this was over.

'Fuck off, Quock!' Sparks showered the cab as he ripped the radio set from the dashboard. He needed quiet in order to concentrate. 'OK, time to party.' He reached for the clockwise rotator lever and froze. The kitchen door had slammed open, and he couldn't believe who staggered out of it. Half eaten lobster in one paw, and a bottle of North Katistonian antifreeze dribbling its contents over the floor in the other, it was the root cause of all evil.

'Fuck a pedalo, it's the midas cat!' He had his nemesis in the same room, and he was driving its damned sister. He could do so much damage. His hand rested on the professor's speech button. The midas cat weaved through the crowds towards him. He had to say something but what?

The kitchen door crashed open again, but this time armed guards swarmed through. They were yelling, but he could only catch a couple of words at best. *Cat. Spy. Escaped.* That was perfect. They thought the midas cat was a Western spy. It kept getting better.

'Yolanda, what are you doing here?' Glassy green eyes glinted in the stripy face. 'Hello. Is there anyone home?'

A white paw flashed across the screen.

'Well, say something.'

Ralph's hand slammed down on the speech button just as his mind went blank. 'B-b-b.'

'Have you got something caught in your throat?' said the midas cat.

'Ladies and gentlemen...' It was the Master of Ceremonies again. 'Please be upstanding for Our Glorious Leader, Kang Dog Wang, and The President of the United States, Marcus L Manx.'

This was his chance, but the stupid bloody tabby one was here now, the one that put him in this situation in the first place.

'Who's the orange bloke with the yellow wig?'

The idiot didn't recognise The Leader of the Free World. Stupid tabby twonk!

'Oh look, it's that fat kid.'

Fat kid? If Kang Dog Wang heard it say that...

'Yolanda, are you all right?'

Ralph stared up at the balcony and back to the midas cat. He had to do something because the guards were closing in.

'As President of the United States, it gives me great pleasure...' The speeches had begun, and he still hadn't acted.

'This'll sort you out.'

Ralph watched as the cat raised a paw. What the hell was it doing?

The paw came down, slapped the professor on the back, and the little craft jolted sideways, tearing free of its moorings. He hit the nitrous button.

Nothing happened. 'Bastard fucker!'

The world upended, and as he looked down, he spotted the speech button jammed in the *on* position. He'd broken free of the brain and was blasting through the ear canal. He had to start the thrusters, or he'd be out of the ear and into the room. Once that happened, he'd get stepped on.

He hit the ignition. The rumbling engines stuttered when the sub bounced off the inner ear. Up ahead was fur and light. Oh bugger, it was the cat's ear hairs. He pushed his thumb down on the button, but the whine of the starter motor slowed to a dragging grind. This was not a good time for the battery to go flat, and he couldn't exactly call for a tow truck.

The sub burst out into the blinding brightness and plummeted towards the table. The drop was only a couple of feet, but he wasn't much bigger than an oversized microbe. Jumping from the Eiffel Tower was about the right scale. That meant one thing. He was about to die.

CHAPTER 8

The Cat

The kitchen door clapped open and across the room Cat could see her Brainiac sister. What was she doing in South Katistonia? She was supposed to be in North Katistonia at some sort of peace meeting.

She weaved through the crowds dropping the empty bottle as she went.

'Cat... spy... escaped...' Some soldiers had burst in looking for a spy cat. She looked around the room. Her and Yolanda were the only cats in the room and neither of them was a spy, so who were they talking about?

'Yolanda, what are you doing here?' Cat stared into her sister's face. Instead of the usual look of deep intelligence, a blank expression stared back. 'Hello. Is there anyone home?' She waved a paw in front of her sister's face. 'Well, say something.'

'B-b-b.'

What the hell was up with her? She usually had so much to say. 'Have you got something caught in your throat?' She dropped the half eaten lobster on the table.

'Ladies and gentlemen...' Some bozo in a red jacket was up on the balcony. Why didn't he shut up? There was a VIP down here, A very important professor.

'Please be upstanding for Our Glorious Leader, Kang Dog Wang, and The President of the United States, Marcus L Manx,' said the red-coated bozo.

'Who's the orange bloke with the yellow wig?' Whoever it was, he shouldn't have used spray tan. That's when Cat spotted a familiar face. 'Oh look, it's that fat kid.' She turned back to her sister who seemed to be in some sort of trance. 'Yolanda, are you all right?' She didn't look all right. She looked as though she'd eaten dog food.

'As President of The United States, it gives me great pleasure...' The perma-tanned plonker was pretending to be the US President. Yeah, as if. She turned back to her sister who looked just as vacant. She knew what to do, though. 'This'll sort you out.'

A hearty slap on the back would dislodge whatever was trapped. She hauled back and landed a paw between the professor's shoulder blades.

Yolanda's eyes went wide, and in a voice loud enough to stop Orange Wig-boy in his tracks, shouted 'bastard fucker!'

The room fell silent. The soldiers had stopped

running, Orange Wig-boy's mouth moved but no sound came out, and the weird fat kid looked as though he wanted to kill someone.

That's when Cat noticed something odd. A tiny pedalo with a little man in it had shot from her sister's ear and was heading towards the table. There was no way she was passing up a toy like that. With a move quicker than sound, she pounced.

The table upended hitting the mini pedalo with a perfect volley, sending it straight towards the weird fat kid.

The sharp smack as the tiny craft connected with the fat kid's eye was followed by a howl of mingled pain and anger. Fat Kid turned to Orange Wig-boy and buried a chubby fist into the centre of his face. *Bugger me, this was good,* thought Cat. The soldiers had forgotten about the spy cat they were chasing and hurtled up the stairs, drawing their guns as they went.

Orange Wig-boy grabbed the fat kid by the ears and bashed his head against the wall whilst shouting 'fire and fury, motherfucker!'

Yolanda shook her head. 'I think it's time for us to leave.'

Cat couldn't disagree. This place was a bit dangerous. 'The kitchen. Let's go out that way.'

It had stopped snowing, and as they exited the alley, Cat smiled. A row of tanks lined the street in front of the palace. There had to be at least a dozen. They wouldn't need all twelve, surely?

She checked out the one at the back. It was unlocked and unattended.

'Are you sure you can drive a tank?' said Yolanda as they settled in.

'How hard can it be?'

Also by Tommy Ellis.

The Midas Cat: The Harrington Collection. A 3000-word short-read. A lorry-load of precious jewels, an Elvis automaton that sings the Postman Pat theme tune, and a hundred-million dollar talking cat. Available as eBook only.

The Midas Cat: The Devil Wears Tabby. If you want to discover the true fate of Lord Lucan, then read on! Available as eBook and paperback.

Short horror stories by Tommy Ellis.

Fast Forward: If you could skip through life's boring bits without ageing, and prison becomes meaningless,what crimes would you be willing to commit? Published by online horror magazine Horla.org.

The Viewing: Buying a house isn't scary...is it? Published by online horror magazine Horla.org

A small request.
If you have a minute to spare, please consider leaving a short review of this book. Your input is appreciated. Thank you.

www.ingramcontent.com/pod-product-compliance
Lightning Source LLC
Chambersburg PA
CBHW071403210526
45465CB00001B/236